Praise for The Last Days of El

"Intimate, alluring, and at times haunting,
The Last Days of Ellis Island imagines the closing
hours of Ellis Island's existence as a gateway for
the hopeful through the eyes of its last caretaker.
Josse examines with care how life, no matter
where you spend it, is a weave of wonderful
moments and sad ones; moments we are
insanely grateful for and moments we wish
with everything within that we could take back.
Eloquently and skillfully rendered."
SUSAN MEISSNER, bestselling author of *A Fall of Marigolds*

"Josse masterfully weaves this moving story of
love and loss around the larger historical context
of the massive wave of immigration arriving in
the US in the early 1900s. Beautifully written,
The Last Days of Ellis Island is compelling
historical fiction with a dash of magical realism
added in."
VINCENT J. CANNATO, author of *American Passage: The History of Ellis Island*

"Combining real and fictional events, Gaëlle
Josse has written a text as visceral as it is
melancholy and vibrant."
Livres Hebdo

"With precise and barbed language, Gaëlle Josse allows us to experience a slice of American history through the movements of a soul preyed upon by its demons. Masterly and urgent!"
Librairie Pages après pages

"Gaëlle Josse visits Ellis Island and constructs an intimate, collective geography, the story of one man intertwined with those of thousands of others. She rejects exaggeration and pathos, instead embracing the joy of invention and facing the crudeness of what happened head-on."
Transfuge

"It's always somewhat pointless to attempt categorization, especially in the impalpable and subjective domain of artistic creation. However, can't we call *The Last Days of Ellis Island* the most beautiful text Gaëlle Josse has ever written, one in which the alchemy of the preceding ones reaches, on a completely different subject, a kind of completion?"
La Croix

"You let yourself be swept along by a narrative that gently oscillates between the supernatural and the unnerving. This literary season's little jewel."
La Vie

"This is the story of the last day of the last guardian of Ellis Island, a place that has for long been the one entryway to the American Dream for thousands of impoverished immigrants. Don't miss this beautiful novel—full of emotion, memory, and vigor."
Femme Actuelle

"A very beautiful novel … about those whom one forgets to thank, those who, because they have been invisible, no longer know how to take back their existence."
L'Alsace

"What is Gaëlle Josse's secret? Every time, we are delighted by her work, and yet this novel has nothing in common with her previous books … The author, in a consistently exquisite style, gives us a work that is not only well-researched and passionate, but also melancholic, and of incomparable power."
Version Femina

"Allows Gaëlle Josse to blend invented emotions and historical truth in a beautiful manner."
Hommes & migrations

"Magnificent. Poignant."
Cosmopolitan

"It's hard not to become John Mitchell during the reading. Gaëlle Josse writes his diary for the last nine working days on Ellis Island with a strong sense of presence and credibility."
Arbetarbladet

"A highly meaningful effort to give voice to people whose destiny has long been forgotten."
Norran

"A novel to be read by anyone who has ever thought about leaving."
Vecernji List

"A breathtaking, beautifully written, melancholy novel—a real gem. The author has brought American society with immigrants from Europe to life, a subject that has lost none of its topicality."
Literair Nederland

"I devoured this gem of a novel, which manages to perfectly capture both a singular moment in time and an entire universe of hope, longing and heartbreak. Brilliantly constructed and beautifully told, *The Last Days of Ellis Island* is a timeless—and timely—exploration of compassion and regret."
CYNTHIA D'APRIX SWEENEY, author of *The Nest*

THE LAST DAYS
OF ELLIS ISLAND

THE
GAËLLE JOSSE
LAST DAYS
OF ELLIS
ISLAND

Translated from the French
by Natasha Lehrer

WORLD EDITIONS

New York, London, Amsterdam

Published in the USA in 2020 by World Editions LLC, New York
Published in the UK in 2020 by World Editions Ltd., London

World Editions
New York / London / Amsterdam

Copyright © Les Editions Noir sur Blanc, 2014
English translation copyright © Natasha Lehrer, 2020
Cover image © Photography Collection, The New York Public
Library
Author portrait © Héloïse Jouanard

Printed by Lake Book, USA

Library of Congress Cataloging in Publication Data is available

ISBN 978-1-64286-071-9

First published as *Le dernier gardien d'Ellis Island* in France in
2014 by Les Editions Noir sur Blanc, Paris

This book was published with the support of the CNL

Twitter: @WorldEdBooks
Facebook: @WorldEditionsInternationalPublishing
Instagram: @WorldEdBooks
www.worldeditions.org

Book Club Discussion Guides are available on our website.

What is this life but the sound of an appalling love?

Louise Erdrich
The Last Report on the Miracles at Little No Horse

We still always paint people against a gold background, like the Italian Primitives. People stand before something indefinite— sometimes gold, sometimes gray. Sometimes they stand in the light, and often with an unfathomable darkness behind them.

Rainer Maria Rilke
Notes on the Melody of Things

(translated by Damion Searls)

Everything that follows took place at sea. On the sea, on two ships, which docked here once upon a time. For me it was as though they never left again, it was the flesh of my flesh and of my soul that they rammed with their anchors and their grapple hooks. Everything I believed to be solid burned to ash. In a few days, I'll be done with this island that has consumed my life. Done with this island of which I am the last guardian and the last prisoner. Done with this island, though I know almost nothing of the world outside. I'll be taking no more than a couple of suitcases and one or two pieces of furniture with me. A few boxes filled with memories. My life.

I have just nine days left before the men from the Federal Immigration Service arrive to officially shut down the Ellis Island immigration station. I have been told that they'll be arriving early, first thing next Friday morning, November 12.

We'll do one last tour of the island together and complete the inventory; I'll hand over the keys to all the doors, gates, warehouses, sheds, desks, and together we'll leave for Manhattan.

Then it'll be time for me to go through the final formalities inside one of those glass and steel buildings whose windows look, from afar, like the countless cells of a beehive, a gray vertical beehive, in a place where I've set foot no more than a dozen times over all these years, and at last I'll be free. At least that's what they'll say to me, with that mixture of pity and envy you might feel for a colleague who, one day at a fixed time, is informed that he is no longer part of the group, is no longer an element of what has become over the years a kind of collective existence, made up of more or less shared concerns and objectives. He must leave the pack, like an old animal moving away to die, while the herd continues on without him. Often this rite of passage is marked by a depressing ceremony. Hackneyed speeches, reminiscences about some shared success, beer, whiskey, a few slaps on the back, and promises of future celebrations that everyone feels obliged to make and forgets at once, and then the person being celebrated weaves his way home, clutching a new fishing line or tool belt. I'll be happy to avoid all that. I have a small apartment waiting for me in Williamsburg in Brooklyn that I inherited from my parents. Three rooms still filled with all their furniture, which I haven't touched; their entire lives embedded between the walls— pictures, ornaments, dishes. Truth be told, I am dreading going back there, I've enough of my own memories without having to deal with theirs, but that's where I was born and I have no other place to go, and I figure it doesn't matter much now.

Nine more days wandering the empty hallways, the disused upper stories and the deserted stairwells, the kitchens, the infirmary, and the Great Hall, where for a long time only my steps have echoed.

Nine days and nine nights until I am to be sent back to the mainland, to the life of men. To a void, as far as I am concerned. What do I know of people's lives today? My own life is already hard enough to fathom, like a book you thought you knew, that you pick up one day and find written in another language. All I have left now is this surprisingly urgent need to write down my story, I don't even know who for, as I sit here in my office that has no purpose anymore, surrounded by so many binders, pencils, rulers, rubber stamps. It's a story that for a few decades has largely been much the same as that of Ellis Island, but it's some events specific to me that I wish to tell here, however difficult it may be. For the rest, I'll leave it up to the historians.

I'm surrounded here by gray: water, concrete, and brick. I've never known any other landscape than that of the Hudson, with its line of skyscrapers that I've watched grow up over the years, climbing, meshing together, stacking up to create the rigid and ever-changing jungle we know today, at its feet the movement of boats and ferries in the bay, and Our Lady of Liberty, or Lady Liberty, as immigrants arriving from Europe sometimes called her when they first caught sight of her on her stone pedestal, majestic in her copper-green robe, face impassive, arm aloft over the water.

Whatever the season, the river is always gray, as if the sun has never been able to illuminate its depths, as if some kind of opaque material beneath the surface prevents it from dipping down into the water to alter its reflection. Only the sky changes. I know all its nuances, from the most intense blue to the softest violet, and all the different shapes of the clouds, wispy, puffy, dappled, each endowing its own character to the new day.

Now all I have authority over is the walls. Grasses and plants have grown wild, taken seed, borne by the wind and the birds. It wouldn't take much for a meadow to grow up here, untamed, along the water's edge, watched over from a distance by a triumphant Liberty tethered securely to her rock. At times it feels as if the entire world has shrunk to the borders of this island. The island of hope and tears. The site of the miracle that destroyed and redeemed, that stripped the Irish peasant, the Calabrian shepherd, the German worker, the Polish rabbi, the Hungarian pencil pusher, of their original nationalities and transformed them into American citizens. Here they are still, a crowd of ghosts floating around me.

I have an inexplicable urge to delve into a past I hoped I would be able to forget, but which it seems I cannot. In a few days I shall be one of those anonymous, modestly dressed retirees, living in an ordinary street in a working-class Brooklyn neighborhood in an apartment the same as a thousand others, taking the bus, greeting my neighbors, feeding my cat, shopping at the grocery store. I know that will be how I appear on the outside, and I know that it will be a complete sham. I have no children, no parents, no family. Nothing but memories, deeply troubling ones. They are so disturbing it's as if all the ghosts in my life awakened as soon as they realized I was leaving, and they will only find peace again once their stories have been told.

My mind is filled with so many images I feel dizzy. Perhaps if I manage to pour my story out onto these pages, embossed with the emblem of the Federal Immigration Service, I will finally be rid of the past. Ellis Island Station. Commissioner. It's all absurd. I'm only trying to keep at bay the shadows that have settled at the foot of my bed and are doggedly insisting on staying put. Nine days. Nine nights. Is that enough time to tell it all?

So. Everything that follows took place at sea, on ships loaded with the poor and the destitute, packed like cattle in steerage, from where they would emerge, dazed, numb, reeling, peering out in the direction of all their hopes and dreams. I can picture them now. Every language was spoken here. It was like a new tower of Babel, but instead of rising up to the sky, the building was low, tethered to the ground. The tower of Babel after it had been destroyed by the God of Genesis. The Babel of desperation and dispersal, the place where everyone was returned to their native language.

Eventually I was able to distinguish between the sounds of all these different languages. I no longer confused them, and I came to recognize characteristics common to those from the same country, even the same region. They didn't all show fear in the same way, and their apprehension was as often translated into silence as into words.

Their faces were clouded with fear and expectation, the dread of saying something wrong, or making some gesture that would mean being forever banned from entering paradise, and yet they had no idea what was expected of them. Many had put on their best clothes for disembarking, ready for the examination that awaited them. Spotless white shirts for the men—it was astonishing they were still in this state after two or three weeks at sea in the filthiest of conditions—and long skirts, fitted jackets, and embroidered bodices for the women. These were their most elaborate outfits, yet they only served to draw attention to the gulf between their world and ours. Men in wide-belted tunics, waistcoats, fur hats, long black kaftans, tweed caps; women, their hair wrapped in headscarves, draped in cascades of necklaces made of colored glass beads or coral. All worlds collided here, and America was the only word they had in common.

Their first examination took place without their knowledge, even though it was the most decisive moment, an ordeal that they had no idea they were undergoing, the final stop on a long and difficult road at the end of which they would either be saved or lost. A long staircase, two flights of stairs they had to climb after depositing their luggage. How many exhausted women did I hear whimper when they saw this staircase rising up in front of them? *Prego, aspetti, signore, ein Moment, bitte ...* Men carrying small children in their arms, the child often asleep with a cheek squashed against the father's shoulder, the mother following behind, out of breath, lifting her skirt so as not to stumble.

As they climbed the stairs they were observed by several line doctors stationed at the top, who leaned over the balustrade, apparently unmoved by these cohorts of utter misery. It took a few seconds—no more than six, it was said—to seal the fate of the new arrivals. Nothing escaped the experienced, professional eye of the line doctor. With a piece of chalk he would write a letter on certain people's clothes.

A letter of the alphabet marked on a jacket or coat corresponded to a particular pathology, either clearly observed, or highly probable. *L* for lungs, *B* for back, *E* for eyes, *H* for heart, *G* for goiter. Passengers thus identified were immediately taken away for further medical examination. The result of the second diagnosis enabled the immigration inspectors to pronounce their verdict: treatment at Ellis Island; pathology unproven; benign pathology; denial of entry into the United States.

Those who passed this stage without a problem found themselves in the Great Hall, which was furnished with rows of wooden benches, where they joined hundreds of other waiting passengers. They were going to be asked twenty-nine questions. Their future depended on their responses. *Sit down here and wait until your name is called.*

Other immigration inspectors called them one by one. *Sit down*, again. A few minutes to answer a series of questions with the help of an interpreter. *What is your final destination in America? Who paid for your passage? How much money do you have? Are you meeting a relative here in America? If so, who, and their address? Have you been in a prison, charity almshouse, or insane asylum? Are you a polygamist? Are you an anarchist? Are you coming to America for a job? What is the condition of your health? Are you deformed or crippled? How tall are you? What is your skin color? What color are your eyes and hair?*

Travelers encountering the Sphinx on the road to Thebes were not bombarded with so many questions! And if those immigrants whose answers were unsatisfactory weren't dismembered alive or devoured by a winged monster with a lion's body, the fate that awaited them was surely no better. At the end of the twenty-ninth question lay either Gehenna or paradise, like that game of dice that children play where you have to avoid landing on certain squares on a colored board, so as not to go backwards, skip your go, or find yourself in prison or at the bottom of a well. Here, there was only one forfeit and it was brutal. The worst that could befall anyone: America slamming the door shut in their face.

These are just memories now. The flow of immigrants dried up a long time ago, and now a steamship docking here is an event. Yet before my eyes these images of the past still stir, present and real. Steamships arriving one after the next, disgorging sometimes thousands of passengers in a single day, with their strange clothes, the way they talked and held themselves, which gradually changed over the years. Lines of people, obedient and anxious, who had to be goaded, hurried, guided, informed, examined. Are you worthy of becoming one of us? What benefit or risk is there for us if we let you in? What do you have to offer us? Some years the station remained open day and night to process the great tide of people. I can picture them still, all the staff who worked there, line doctors and nurses, tired and haggard, standing to face these waves of men and women who were even more exhausted, and had so much more at stake.

After 1924, thanks to President Coolidge's successive immigration laws, the process began to change. There were fewer people to inspect, since quotas were being applied to all foreign nations, and it was now our consuls in the immigrants' countries of origin who were responsible for the initial examination of every visa application. Anyone who was allowed to board a boat would not, in principle, be turned back upon arrival. That meant our role diminished, for we were now no more than the last links in an immense chain designed to keep out anyone who had somehow managed to dodge the checks or circumvent the procedures.

I was never, or rarely ever, in direct contact with the new arrivals. They had left everything behind, were exhausted and debilitated by the voyage, and it was only the hope of a new life that gave them the strength to remain standing. There were many different teams of people: interpreters, inspectors, guards, and medical staff. I was responsible for ensuring that everything was in working order in the sleeping quarters, kitchens, infirmary, sanitary areas, and isolation zones. Here was where they slept, ate, washed, defecated, wept, waited, talked, held each other, struggled to calm wailing, confused children, tried not to think too much, hoped, and yearned.

For forty-five years—I've had plenty of time to count them—I observed the arrival of all those men, women, and children, dignified and disoriented, in their best clothes and bathed in perspiration, exhaustion, and bewilderment, struggling to make sense of a language of which they knew not a single word. They carried all their dreams inside their luggage, packed inside the trunks, canteens, baskets, suitcases, bags, carpets, and blankets that contained everything they had brought with them from their previous life; and then there was everything they had sealed up deep inside their hearts to try to keep themselves from caving in to the anguish of separation, the pain of calling up faces they would never see again. They had to move on, adapt to another life, another language, different signs and customs, unfamiliar foods, a new climate. Learn, learn fast and never look back. I have no idea how many of them fulfilled their dreams, how many found themselves brutally cast into a daily life that was barely any improvement on the one they had escaped. It was too late to think about it, theirs was an exile without return.

I remember the day, many years ago now, when the meaning of a few lines of verse, imprinted on my memory since childhood, suddenly became clear, a little like finding an object in your pocket that seems to be of no use, you hold onto it without quite knowing why, and then one day it reveals its purpose.

By the rivers of Babylon, there we sat down, yea, we wept, when we remembered Zion. We hanged our harps upon the willows in the midst thereof.

For there they that carried us away captive required of us a song; and they that wasted us required of us mirth, saying, Sing us one of the songs of Zion.

How shall we sing the Lord's song in a strange land?

This psalm of exile came back to me, suddenly, with extraordinary exactitude; it felt like I'd stumbled against something in a hallway in the middle of the night, and only then remembered it was there. The Sunday service, when I was a child. Reverend Hackson, with his sparrow-like silhouette in a black habit, his halting gait and jerky movements; I can still hear the reedy voice muffled in his chest that grew a little louder with each sentence until it was like a surge, a great swell that every time I was convinced would never end. In the winter cold, inside the poorly heated church, my hair still damp from my Sunday morning scrub, wedged into a jacket that every week seemed to have shrunk a little more, I could hardly wait for the service to be over, and then the weekly ritual of beef pie for Sunday lunch, so I could run off and play baseball. The words of the psalm were completely incomprehensible to me.

In fact, when it came to rivers, I didn't know much apart from the industrial, gray Hudson, and I didn't see how you could hang harps on nonexistent willow trees. All I had was a vague image of candy canes dangling from the branches of the Christmas tree that my parents used to take the trouble to put up for me every year in our tiny living room. And if the land of the exodus was a desert, I couldn't see how there could be rivers there either. The biblical words barely touched me, and I gave up going to church as soon as I could duck out of that particular Sunday obligation. I guess words sometimes dig mysterious chambers deep inside you, and what you thought was buried, forgotten, or lost forever insists on resurfacing out of the blue.

It's like they seize hold of you, and you're entirely defenseless. At Ellis Island the harps had fallen silent. At last I understood.

Time has stopped here, everyone has moved on with their lives, only I am still here, standing on the dock, the last witness to these manifold destinies, the hours and days of transit that definitively altered the countenance of so many people's lives. *Welcome to America!* The anxious wait for the benediction, the baptismal certificate, the permit, the document that allowed you to become an American, from now until the hour of your death. And then the golden door would swing open. Yet for so many the door creaked, and they would have to oil it for generations to come. For the truth is, no miracle awaited them here, except whatever they made for themselves. Hard work and poor pay for the lucky ones, a squalid, noisy apartment to live in, but freedom, and the chance of a new beginning.

These scenes took place in different areas of the main reception building, between the four ornamental turrets faced in brick and limestone, with onion domes that I imagine to many recalled the churches of their native lands. As for the rest, we are surrounded by water, glass, and metal. We have no other horizon.

11 O'CLOCK, IN THE EVENING.
Over time, the role of the station evolved, as did my own as my duties changed. I began here as an immigration inspector, responsible for directing the arrival of this human tide of immigrants clutching their possessions as they disembarked from the barge that ferried them over from Battery Park at the southern tip of Manhattan. This was where the steamships docked to let off the first- and second-class passengers, their papers in order, having already been checked on board, the men in overcoats with fur collars, and the women in hats with veils, and fine leather shoes.

My knowledge of the procedures and the precise layout of the site, the suggestions I made to streamline the process, my reliability and general aptitude, meant that I rose rapidly through the ranks and was soon promoted to supervising other people and dealing with increasingly complex technical and administrative issues. I had been deputy to the commissioner for some time when my predecessor was posted elsewhere, and it was simpler to offer me his position than to appoint a new commissioner, who would probably have been aghast at the idea of moving here. I wasn't expecting it and was already getting used to the idea of working for a new boss, all the whims and habits to which I'd have to adapt. I accepted the promotion, trying not to show too much surprise. And I soon discovered that the exercise of power and authority, however minimal and insignificant, requires a certain silence and solitude, and, when it comes to the expression of feelings, reserve. These barriers suited me perfectly. I assumed the role.

At first glance, with its corridors and staircases so similar to the walkways of the vessels from which the immigrants had just disembarked, Ellis Island must have seemed like a labyrinth. I am probably the only person familiar with all its dark corners, for the other people who worked there had only a partial view of it, their own specific domain. Throughout the main building floated the persistent smell of Lysol, which I grew so used to I no longer noticed it. I was always scrupulous about hygiene and disinfection. It was, I confess, almost an obsession, but with passengers arriving off the boats infested with lice, vermin, and all kinds of sicknesses, it was vital. As I was only too painfully aware.

The immigration services needed people like me, I suppose, reliable and efficient. And for reasons that I may perhaps reveal later in these pages, if I succeed in being as candid as I hope, for this is all starting to weigh heavily on me, I always declined to leave the island. Who else but I, who had lived here so long, would have been able to understand the layout of this maze? Over the years, and with the war, immigration dwindled and the flood of newcomers was succeeded first by military troops in training and then by political prisoners awaiting deportation. For some, I opened the golden door; for others, I slammed it shut on their hopes; for others still, I was a prison warden, a passing shadow, silent and severe, of whom the worst was always assumed. Serving your country sometimes takes an unexpected turn, and one is not always master of the face one shows to others.

So now Ellis Island is closing its doors, like a flophouse forced out of business, or a hotel with no custom, being too far from passing traffic, or a jail with no prisoners, or all those at once. The government took the decision with the idea of turning a page on this history, and of refurbishing the island's buildings in anticipation of the seventieth anniversary of the statue, which has enchanted the world since it was first raised in the bay in 1886. What an emblem, what a work of art, this gift from France! How strangely things turn out. In any case, over the next few years no effort will be spared in the planning of lavish celebrations worthy of a symbol that beguiles the entire world. *God bless America!* I can only imagine the ceremonies, commemorations, official speeches, anthems, marching bands, bugles and drums, heel taps, right faces, parades with flags fluttering in the wind that will take place, one after the next. Perhaps I will be invited, one relic among so many others, to don my uniform for the occasion and escort eminent visitors as they gather in this place through which more than twelve million immigrants from all over Europe have passed since it first opened. Maybe I will be asked to satisfy their curiosity about how things were done, and to share some poignant anecdotes. They may be assured that I have more than enough of those. But is it even possible, in these desolate spaces, between the broken windowpanes, deserted dormitories, and worm-ridden piers, to imagine the things that once took place here?

Anyway, this is no time for such thoughts. I am alone here now in this forsaken place; the last members of staff and the last transiting passenger left a few days ago. I feel like a captain standing at the bow of his sinking ship, but, truth be told,

I was shipwrecked long ago, and I do not know now if leaving will be an ordeal or a deliverance. Ellis Island's last guest has departed, a Norwegian sailor, ginger-haired and taciturn, a colossus who spent his time prowling around the buildings while he waited for the court to decide his fate. Finally the decision came down and he was released, welcomed onto American soil, and sent on his way.

I'd grown used to the pungent odor of his tobacco, and we would exchange a few words when we passed each other during our respective wanderings, each conscious of being all but forgotten here on this deserted island at the edge of the world, locked in our respective roles and committed to playing them right to the end: the foreign suspect and the camp guard. No, I exaggerate: some nights I'd offer him a drink and we might play a game of chess, violating the most basic rules of my position, though I couldn't say if I did it as a kindness more for his sake or for mine. Sometimes solitude weighs you down. When he left we shook hands like equals;

then he headed off without a backward glance to his new home, kitbag slung over his shoulder and cigarette hanging off his lip. He was free. He boarded the boat and left for Manhattan. Arne Peterssen. My last prisoner.

The curious story of this taciturn Viking has mostly faded from my memory, like so many others, and the ones that stick are not the most joyful. Why did Peterssen end up staying on Ellis Island so long, in a silent standoff like a kind of dance or duel, in which each participant was trying to move away from his adversary rather than advance towards him? I seem to remember that he had been involved in a brawl on board ship, whose hazy circumstances the investigation tried to unravel. An officer was involved, and for whatever reason, this was not something that could be pardoned. The Norwegian navy was only too happy to let go of this ill-disciplined specimen who had requested American citizenship. His application inevitably meant additional investigations and evidence to be crosschecked, that is to say a great quantity of official paperwork on headed paper, stamped every which way. And so a single ordinary evening, during which vast quantities of alcohol were consumed in one of those harbor bars where women in black stockings offer up their bodies to quell some desperate, sad, swiftly satisfied desire, was transformed into an endless legal proceeding turning on irreconcilable arguments. Apart from this one incident, Peterssen's record was spotless, and he seemed to have always been loyal and competent. Magnanimous, America chose to pardon this lapse, which did not, in the end, concern her. It turned out that the officer in question had his share of responsibility in the brawl with the sailor that night, in one of those places where the hostesses must have witnessed countless such spectacles.

The few workers still stationed on the island left immediately after him, in his wake you might say, only too eager to jump ship, to escape the ghosts and start their lives over. Richard Green, a cook, and

Robert Patterson, a warden and handyman. It's a relief. My solitude is now complete. I've been waiting for this moment for so long, that I might finally start to write. Robert, with his quiet step, despite his size, his face creased like a sheet of paper that has been crumpled into a ball, and a disturbing scar barely concealed by his dark beard, had the art of appearing out of nowhere at any moment. I always felt like I was being watched; his wrestler's build intimidated me, and without the authority conferred on me by a title that demanded at least a modicum of respect, I think I would have been a little afraid of him. Richard cooked for years for passengers who were obliged to remain on Ellis Island for various reasons and lengths of time—on medical grounds, or due to some issue regularizing their status, or while awaiting further interrogation. He was cheerful and sociable, and had a curious habit of ending every sentence with an inexplicable burst of laughter, perhaps intended to mask his shyness and embarrassment; but the progressive winding down of activity on Ellis Island eventually crushed his propensity to laugh over even the most trivial thing. I could never bring myself to eat what he prepared, unidentifiable morsels in brown sauces kept warm for hours that congealed on the plate in less time than it took to describe what it was. In comparison to the unsavory dishes and meager rations served on board ship, I can see that for the newcomers his food, plentiful and hot, must have seemed like manna from heaven. Ever since Richard's arrival, in order not to upset him, I took to claiming that I was on a strict diet that I had to follow because of my supposed delicate digestion. I've kept up the habit. Even today, I'm satisfied with coffee, bacon, eggs, cookies, and fruit. With age, the body's needs dwindle. Only my desire for solitude continues to grow.

In a few days I, too, will be leaving this place, so melancholy and so familiar. And I shall have to bid farewell to the grassy plot where Liz has lain for so many years. The tree I planted on her grave gives shade now, which is how I measure the passing of time. There are other graves in this enclosed space, for people died here just as they do everywhere. There is one in particular I avoid; one of the gray stones marked with a cross and etched with a name and a date is located a little away from the others, as I had requested. It is almost entirely covered in weeds now: long, supple grasses that shiver in the wind, dark-green clover with mauve flowers, buttercups, their incongruous color almost indecent in this setting; it was as if the vegetation was trying to bury what had happened for a second time. I have cleared my desk, everything is neatly filed in glass-fronted cabinets, with the records of each and every immigrant sorted according to year and in alphabetical order, and a record of every steamship, as well as all medical records, and the maintenance and logistics ledgers. Only one is missing, the *Cincinnati*, the steamship from Naples that docked on April 21, 1923. I made that boat disappear. I only wish I could erase it from my memory as well.

This morning, as every morning, I did my tour of inspection, even though there is almost nothing left to check—but I still have this job to do, my daily round of the site. If nothing was expected of me, why have they waited till today to bring me back to the mainland to rejoin the living? They could have simply sent someone over when required. Every morning, notepad in hand, I walk around the island and write down what will go in my report. This is written up into a weekly summary that I send on to the federal bureau, where a division head might cast a distracted glance over it before handing it to a secretary to file with the rest. That's what they pay me for. To maintain the place in decent repair, notify whatever is necessary, and send my report. Nothing else now.

As I do every morning, I visited the little cemetery where Liz waits for me. Maybe it's a foolish thought, but that is what I believe. I shall have to tell her that my daily visits are coming to an end. As soon as I can, I'll ask for her grave to be moved to the cemetery in South Brooklyn where my parents are buried. It'll be a lengthy process, but I don't want to leave her here alone. I've already requested authorization; it's the only favor I am asking before I leave.

Liz was my guiding light. Nothing triumphant or blinding like the light that is brandished for all eternity by Lady Liberty. My poor Liz, the very idea would have made her smile. No, she was mellow, constant, serene. We were married only a few years. Too little time, but is the intensity of an experience measured by its duration? The interminable pace of my life today has no significance for me anymore. I get up, work, go to bed and wrangle with the memories I have tried to build walls to keep out. I barely manage it, and anyway it will all come to an end one day or another.

Liz worked here as a nurse, and we lived in the lodgings I still occupy, originally just a single room for employees who lived on the premises. When I'd gotten my promotion I was given permission to knock down the dividing walls to the adjacent rooms to make a more spacious apartment. Liz had so little time to enjoy it, and the images I've held on to of those years are of our one room, ingeniously arranged by Liz into different areas: a small bathroom, a tiny kitchen, and a dining nook. That meant we didn't have to join the rest of the staff in the evening in the noisy dining room, and it gave us a little privacy, so sorely lacking in this place.

When I met her I was already employed here, but in fact I had known her for a long time without having ever paid her the slightest attention. She was the younger sister of Brian MacPherson, my closest friend. I was an only child. Brian and I spent all our childhood and adolescence together, lived in the same neighborhood, and went to the same school. Our mothers looked alike, energetic and solid, their bodies grown stout with the years, wrapped in dark aprons, strands of gray hair escaping from their untidy buns. They were never slow to lay down a smack on a child they caught dawdling, and for nothing in the world would either of them ever forget to put on her hat, fixed with a long pin tipped by a fake pearl, when she went to sing in church on a Sunday morning.

I must have seen Liz dozens of times since I first became friends with Brian. She was a little younger than us, in other words entirely uninteresting. I paid her no more notice than I might have a pet or an umbrella stand. I might have a vague memory of a girl in braids and long socks, silently moving around their cluttered and cramped apartment.

Brian and I spent our childhood together, with its games, fights, and cruelty, and then our adolescence, talking about girls and fantasizing about the dancing girls whose photographs we saw in magazines, with their shapely arms, ringlets, and smoldering eyes. Brian started out as a clerk in a Manhattan insurance company, the New York Life Insurance Company, which he would say as if it were all one word, catching his breath slightly after. I found a job at the Federal Immigration Service. They were taking on people to deal with the endless waves of people washing up at Ellis Island. I took a job that wasn't very defined, the main thing was I had to be there, sleep there, and obey orders. I could read, write, and count; I was pretty resourceful and I didn't balk at working hard. After the first few weeks it became clear that I was good at dealing with a group of men and knew how to garner respect.

It was when I went to spend a Sunday with Brian's parents on Heyward Street that I met Liz, or rather I met her again, like a new version of herself. She opened the door for me—*Hey, John, you're late already*—and smiled at me without apparent surprise, as if I were a relative she didn't need to make any effort for, or someone she was expecting whose appearance was the most natural thing in the world. I had to say that this smiling young woman in a pretty dress who welcomed me bore no resemblance to the little girl with scrappy braids and woolen socks. Brian was, as usual, taking his time getting ready, so she had me wait with her and asked about my work as if nothing in the world interested her more. She told me she was about to finish nursing school and then start looking for a job. More than her slender figure and her pretty face, I think it was her eyes that struck me the most that day, her direct, attentive way of listening without shyness or flattery, flirtatiousness or superiority. The way she listened to me, it was as if I were handing her the keys to the universe, and when Brian eventually appeared I had to make a considerable effort to end the conversation, which did not escape his notice.

I started going back to Brooklyn as often as I could, and it was no longer Brian I wanted to see. He was courting a young woman whose job was selling perfume on 7th Avenue in Manhattan, and he was gracious enough to let me woo his sister and spare me his comments. Maybe it amused him, but I suspected he was keeping an eye on my developing love affair with the younger sister he so adored with more attention than he cared to admit. I realized later that this affection, which he managed to keep lighthearted and teasing, in fact concealed a concerned tenderness. I understood from his allowing me to court her that he trusted me, but also that our friendship would not withstand Liz's tears if I were the cause. I loved Liz, and desired her. It felt as if she had been waiting for me all her young life, and it seemed to me inconceivable that she could be destined for anyone else.

8 O'CLOCK IN THE EVENING.

I asked her to marry me one day in June. She flushed the color of the cherries on her hat and burst into tears. That was when I knew she was in love with me too. My mother was fond of her, though she lamented how slender she was—*She's real skinny, that sweetheart of yours*—and my father, who by then was working on the streetcars, having driven a hansom cab most of his life, contented himself with a growl—*Your honey is pretty cute.*

It was 1915. Europe was at war and America had not yet entered the conflict. We had a simple wedding, with flowers, sparkling wine, tears, and many warm embraces. Brian was more moved than he wanted to admit judging by the number of times he poked me in the ribs over the course of the day. He sported a pale gray tie for the occasion and had brought his sweetheart, his almost-fiancée, a young woman who worked as a salesgirl in a hat shop; she had a strident, nasal voice, and was wrapped in a dark feather boa and enough perfume for all the women there. She was the latest in line of Brian's salesgirls, they all worked in some boutique or other selling hats or jewelry, were all equally strident and nasal, prickly and perfumed. The young lady of the moment, Daisy, had this habit of wrinkling her nose when she laughed; I imagine someone had once told her it was a charming mannerism, or that it made her look like some vaudeville starlet.

It was before Prohibition, which meant we were legally permitted to attain the state of blessed cheer and universal love that a few glasses confer. Our fathers were already fast friends and busy making plans for future Sundays, which, when they could, they liked to spend out of the house. Our mothers confined themselves to keeping a watch on them out of the corners of their eyes, dreading the moment when their cheerful good humor would open the floodgates to lewd jokes and wild laughter.

It was precisely at this time of restrained festivity that we enjoyed the greatest and probably the only luxury of our lives: a few days' honeymoon in Sterling Forest, fifty miles from New York, in a small hotel by a lake. We boarded the train for Tuxedo at Penn Station, me carrying our two suitcases and Liz following as if I were beating a path with a machete through virgin jungle, beheading snakes and howler monkeys at every step. Upon our arrival, a horse-drawn carriage took us through Sterling Forest to Evergreen Lodge, where for the first time I proudly signed the guestbook *Mr. and Mrs. Mitchell.*

I had never seen so many trees in all my

life, the clear, dark outline of pines as far as the eye could see, the water a dazzling, icy blue. Liz observed, asked questions, gathered wildflowers that she reluctantly left behind when we returned to the hotel, where we ate alone in the dining room, overwhelmed by everything we had seen that day. Let me simply say that Liz was curious about matters of the flesh and responded eagerly to my ardor. I was a happy man. That in my life I have known such moments remains, so many years later, an inexhaustible source of wonderment. When we returned, I succeeded in having her hired as a nurse on Ellis Island, where she joined the hardworking medical staff. She worked in the infirmary that took in the sick, the wounded, and the crippled, and she also assisted the medical officers in carrying out compulsory medical examinations of newly arrived female immigrants.

They were looking for lice, evidence of trachoma, or the early stages of pregnancy; they might listen to a worrying cough, change a dressing, disinfect a wound, hand out thermometers and medication, or even occasionally assist a surgeon during an operation. The sufferings of the body are endless. Liz performed this demanding work without showing the slightest disgust or impatience, with a gentleness for which she was criticized by some of her nursing colleagues, who saw her kindness as little more than a waste of time, given the lines that stretched far beyond the glass doors of their station.

Often, back in our room late at night, she was drained, exhausted, and close to tears, distraught about some hopeless case or tragic story she had heard about or intuited. I, who had always been happy simply to keep the station running smoothly, was discovering with her the meaning of abject misery, separation, and hope. I was learning to discern a person's fate, their history, in a veiled expression or a hesitant step. *Oh, John, if you only knew ...* Sometimes she couldn't say anything more, so I had to take my time, despite all the other things I'd have liked to talk about, to wait for her words to come, without forcing them, because it was essential that my dear sweet Liz rid herself, before the day ended, of the burden of all the things she'd heard, impotent and helpless; and it was only after she told me everything that she would at last relax a little, show me the gestures of affection I was hoping for, and receive mine.

All this lasted just a few years, barely five short years, and despite the challenging episodes that we were witness to, we were truly happy. Then tragedy struck. When the *Germania* docked here on September 27, 1920, the captain immediately informed us that there had been several deaths during the crossing. The doctor on board had been discreet enough not to frighten the 2,400 passengers, three-quarters of whom were traveling in the notoriously overcrowded steerage. Five bodies hastily wrapped in sheets had been quietly thrown overboard after dark during the crossing, and he had begun to panic. I can still see his nervous gestures, the uneasy way he spoke, his anxious expression. An epidemic on board. Typhus. Contagion. Ten new cases had been isolated in the quarantine area.

Liz was on duty over those days. She hardly left her post and had her meals brought to the infirmary that had been transformed into an isolation ward. She spent one night on a folding bed, along with a colleague, trying to soothe the sick as best she could. One night, not long after, she complained of a headache, which was unusual for her, and abdominal pain. Desperately worried, I went to fetch Doctor Graham, whose calm and compassion I appreciated. Initially he was furious at being woken when he had just finished his duties and was desperate for a few hours' sleep, but he turned pale when I described her symptoms. *What are you saying?* He ran after me down the corridors towards our room and immediately placed Liz in quarantine. She smiled and told me not to worry. I was allowed to see her briefly the next day, when she had finally fallen asleep after hours of fighting a fever, vomiting, and diarrhea. I couldn't bring myself to wake her and simply held her hand and stroked her forehead. I thought her drawn expression was easing, her face seemed a little less tense. I stayed for a long time at her bedside, with no awareness of time, holding her hand in mine, hoping to sense some slight pressure in response. I thought I felt it, though I had no idea that would be our last exchange and our farewell. I was persuaded to go and rest awhile. A few hours later, the sound of knocking woke me. Doctor Graham was at the door, his hair slick with perspiration, his spectacles pushed up onto his forehead. *I'm so sorry about Liz, sir. So terribly sorry. It's over.*

When I reached the infirmary I was greeted by tearful nurses and heavy silence. How deeply Liz was loved. I had always known it, and here I was reminded of it one last time. Someone asked me if I would like to see her. At that moment, I truly wished I had never been born.

Because of the risk of contagion, the funeral was held almost immediately. My parents and Liz and Brian's parents, overwhelmed with grief, crossed the bay to Ellis Island. Liz's mother regarded me with unconcealed hostility. In her eyes it was I who was responsible for her daughter's death, I was guilty of having brought her to this sewer that gave shelter to the dregs of the earth. She seemed afraid that she was going to be attacked by germs and bacteria. I saw her flinch from touching anything and she carefully lifted her skirt and held it close to her. I couldn't blame her. Maybe she was right. She kept casting suspicious, appalled looks at everything around her. Brian was there, not even trying to hold back his tears. He'd come alone; Daisy, whom he'd married, was pregnant, and he didn't want to force her to travel in circumstances that could not have been more difficult.

The ceremony was brief and low-key; there were bouquets and flowers tied simply with ribbons, placed on the coffin one by one, each person awkwardly scanning the others' faces, eyes lowered and ill at ease. I refused the sober black cloth with silver tassels that I'd been offered to drape over the coffin: Liz loved color. Most of the station personnel were there, except for those who couldn't leave their posts. The doctors and nurses stood together, their expressions both more inconsolable and more impenetrable than the others. Their grief was sincere, I had no doubt, and accompanied by the abrupt realization that Liz's fate might have been theirs, and could indeed still be one day.

I staggered as the coffin was lowered into the ground, steadied by two thick ropes held by officers. I heard the wood as it touched the ground, and the ropes were pulled up, relieved of their burden. I don't know who it was who took my arm to draw me away, but I do recall following him like a child.

Immediately after the funeral, two orderlies came to collect Liz's soiled bedlinen and laundry for burning. I found that more unbearable than the funeral. I was stunned, devastated, in shock. The infirmary witnessed three further deaths in the days that followed. I had to log everything, including Liz's death, in my daily reports. I would not wish such suffering on anyone. At just twenty-seven she was gone. I had never thought such a thing possible. I know that it was just one injustice among many, one tragic event among so many others, but it was mine.

After Liz's death, I rarely left Ellis Island. During the first few months I made an effort to visit her parents in Williamsburg. I went feeling that I was paying off a debt, because I knew they expected it of me. Her mother's hostility towards me had given way to a certain compassion. They had a need to talk about their daughter, about the happiness she had brought them that they would never know again. They portrayed a woman who really only existed for them. My Liz had little in common with the person they described; the childhood scenes they brooded on and their memories frozen in time meant nothing to me. I held on to the image of a gentle, intense, loving, and joyful young woman. It was an image that was impossible to share.

Brian and Daisy, meanwhile, tried to

support me with their presence and affection; at the same time they understood that the spectacle of their relationship and their happiness, multiplied tenfold by the birth of their son Harry, was too much for me to bear. I gradually withdrew from Brooklyn and its busy streets, its brownstones, workshops, and small stores, leaving behind my youth and my past. I realized it was a relief.

Liz and Daisy were about as different from one another as two women could possibly be. I was only too aware, every time we went out together as we often did, of the limited scope of their conversation, how different their concerns were, how superficial their exchanges, and I sensed their mutual discomfiture when, having exhausted every possible subject they might have had in common, a forlorn silence descended between them.

In the summer, like so many from Brooklyn and the rest of New York, we were drawn to Coney Island. Coney Island and its round-the-clock amusements, Luna Park, and the endless boardwalk along the ocean.

Brian, with his steady hand and limber hips, was unbeatable at bowling. I held my own very respectably at the shooting range, and we gave our wives the pleasure of choosing from among the prizes whatever trinket they desired. Daisy loved the freak show, the distorting mirrors, and the ghost train, and she would find any excuse to giggle and shriek, to Liz's intense irritation. In high spirits, and absolutely ravenous by then, we'd grab a Nathan's Famous hot dog and a glass of beer. At those moments, I was convinced our friendship would last forever.

Brian and I, bound by our shared history, were always so happy to see each other, even though our friendship was more about what we had gone through together than what we had in common. Over time we had grown more and more different; I envied him his carefree nature, his ability to live in the moment, to forget the rest of the world and simply enjoy himself. His work at New York Life bored him to death, but he'd just shrug his shoulders and insist on *looking on the bright side*, as he repeated often. In this respect, Daisy was very much like him, but she didn't have a tenth of his generosity and instinctive kindness towards others.

I rarely went into Manhattan after Liz died, as if the two miles that separated Ellis Island from Battery Park presented a greater obstacle than the whole of the Atlantic Ocean and its icebergs and storms. This distance, which every time became more apparent, more tangible, as if the mainland were pushing me away a little more at every attempt I made to approach it, made me realize how much it was Liz who had forged my links with the world. She was my intermediary, my intercessor, my translator, and my interpreter. Unlike me, she loved the city, the parade of people, the store windows, streetcars, broad avenues, all the bustle, as if it were a single, extraordinary, gigantic performance with multiple scenes and sets, a Broadway show split into parts, as unchanging as it was constantly reinvented. How she must have loved me to have come and shared my life on this dreary little island!

Whenever we had a day off, whatever the weather, she'd insist we leave first thing in the morning so we could make the most of the day. I wonder now if she felt a recurrent need to verify that there was still an elsewhere, a different life that was lighter, more joyful than ours, that would cleanse her of the week's sorrows, allow her to erase all the difficult moments, breathe different air, and perhaps just forget, for a few hours, our lives on this raft.

Liz's true passion was musicals, the Ziegfeld Follies especially. The greatest pleasure I could give her was to buy her tickets for a show. You had to see the joy, the childish delight that lit up her face. As soon as the tickets arrived, she'd slip them carefully into the frame of the large gilded mirror in our bedroom above the dresser, so she could keep looking at them, her excited anticipation lit up afresh every time she caught a glance of them, right up until the day of the performance. When we arrived home after the show she'd put the tickets away carefully, and keep the program to read over and over for weeks on end. She daydreamed about Marilyn Miller, Fred Astaire, about the chorus lines, the songs, her favorite tap-dance numbers. The thing I loved most about the shows was the utter enchantment that lit up her face, though I certainly didn't scorn their cheerful artifice and frivolity.

We had our own routine at the New Amsterdam Theater on 42nd Street off of Times Square, where the Ziegfeld Follies were playing at the time. I can still see the narrow frontage on the street, so narrow that it was impossible to imagine the immense auditorium, which you reached by a long, curving corridor that led to the sacred space. I must admit I was more sensitive to the beauty of the place than to the musicals and comedies that were staged there, with their mawkish, silly, contrived plots that were only made watchable thanks to the breathtaking staging, a riot of backdrops and costumes, and the actors' talent.

There was a huge stage, with tiered seating, private boxes, the orchestra pit, and a profusion of gilding, frescoes, pillars, and painted panels depicting ingenuous allegories of Deception and Truth, Love, Melancholy, and Chivalry. For a few hours, here was a place and a time that allowed me to forget everything else, with the warmth of Liz's body next to mine, closer than daily life allowed—apart from when we slept, but then of course we were unconscious of each other. I would watch her profile, her hair, the nape of her neck, imagining her expression in the semi-darkness. Astonishment, laughter, surprise, tears. She experienced every scene, every moment, as intensely as if she herself were on stage and her life depended on it.

At the end of the show we had other rituals, first a drink, then dinner or a snack, depending on how late it was. I knew she'd still be lost in the story we had just watched. I'd wait for her to regain her foothold in the real world and let her be the first to speak. I always urged her to bring home a pastry, or something; I was worried about how slender she was, though I never dared admit it to her. Despite the pleasures of our intimate life, her stomach remained resolutely flat. I refrained from making any comment or asking her about it, for fear she would take it as a reproach. I would have hated to add to what I imagined to be her sadness, and I had come to see our relationship as entirely self-contained.

After her death, my personal geography, the whole way I comprehended places, was redrawn. Without her, Broadway was merely despair, an unbearable din, and it would never have occurred to me to go into any of the cafés or restaurants we used to frequent. The city without her was without purpose, it no longer had any meaning for me. As for my efforts to maintain the tenuous ties that bound me to Brooklyn, they faded very fast. I stayed on Ellis Island, and made do with the radio and the newspapers to keep me abreast of what was happening in the world.

10 O'CLOCK IN THE EVENING.

In the months following Liz's death, my work saved me, or at least kept me from sinking into complete despair. On the island there was no place or face that did not remind me of her gentle presence. I dwelled inside my memories of her, as if she were still by my side, her cool hand ruffling my hair, with her thoughtful concern, her optimism, her radiant kindness. I only had to close my eyes to see her face and hear her voice. I could stay like that for hours, delaying the moment when I would have to face reality again, her absence digging furrows of grief deep within me.

The endless activity on Ellis Island, and the many decisions to be made, instructions to be given, and reports to be written, were now my exclusive focus, and I took to delaying as long as possible the moment when I would find myself alone in what had been our home together, in front of the gilded wooden mirror where every morning Liz, her arms raised in a graceful gesture that managed to be both casual and precise, would wind her hair into a chignon that she'd fix with a few hairpins in a fruitless bid to keep her fine hair off of her temples and the back of her neck.

One unbearably sad evening, in a furious outburst of grief, I took hold of the mirror and unhooked it from the wall. Tottering beneath its weight, I found myself on the ground, bleeding and in tears, surrounded by shards of glass, every one of which held within it the vanished reflection of Liz.

Those months and years were very hard. I barely registered the changing seasons, cared nothing about what I ate or drank. I tired myself out working from dawn to dusk. I kept a watchful eye on everything. There were a few major projects to oversee: maintenance, repairs, cleaning, an extension to the building. I was always dealing with construction workers who came from Long Island, Brooklyn, the Bowery, all over the Five Boroughs, and sometimes stayed for several weeks. I was in charge of coordinating laborers, painters, electricians, and plumbers, keeping tabs on every detail. I was punctilious, demanding, and insufferable. Did people realize that all the additional chaos I was purposefully creating was for the sole purpose of exhausting and distracting myself, diverting my thoughts away from Liz by absorbing my attention every minute of every day? It was a pitiful defense, but I was incapable of inventing any other.

I limited my interactions and conversations with the staff at the station, unable to cope with what I read in everybody's eyes, whether pained incomprehension or sympathetic pity. I couldn't bear it. I knew that they all, to different degrees, had their own memories of Liz, and that was a part of them that I couldn't bear to think about. This reaction might sound odd, even absurd; perhaps I should have been glad that Liz had mattered to other people and that her memory continued, gently, to sweeten our lives, but that wasn't how I saw things.

Little by little, I began to understand that I had locked myself inside my silence and pain and made it impossible for me to see or accept the slightest sign of concern or sympathy directed towards me. It wasn't a question of pride, not at all. It was simply a complete inability to allow the slightest emotion to show, for fear that I would fall apart for good. The series of events that came to pass a few years later, taking me by complete surprise, destroyed in an instant this miserable barrier that I had so patiently constructed.

I heard occasional, though only vague, rumors of various momentous events that left their mark on the country. The pitilessness of prohibition, clashes between the police and the Sicilian mafia, stakeouts, the bloody settling of accounts; later the misery and tragedy of the Great Depression, Black Thursday on Wall Street, which unfolded almost directly facing where I sat, farmers' livelihoods destroyed in the Dust Bowl, hunger, unemployment, protest marches down Manhattan's avenues—all this reached me like the echo of a world that was no longer mine. Sure, the world had changed, I saw the advertisements in the newspapers, how different everything now was. Shingled hair, cherry-red lips, and complicated bodices had given way to breasts squashed under dresses with wide, petalled skirts, bare arms and legs, and bold expressions. Men seemed taller now, broader in the shoulder, more at ease in their suits, their smiles, and their demeanors. Everyone was buying cars, fridges, domestic appliances. I heard new music on the radio, and read about movies I'd never see. I noted all these developments without lingering on them, the way one apprehends information without reflection, like a barely perceptible change of scenery. I think it's called time passing.

Then it was wartime, again, though by then I was too old for the draft. It affected me only indirectly, but with a particular intensity. Brian and Daisy suffered the terrible pain of losing Harry, their only son, on June 6, 1944, at Omaha Beach. I went straight over to see them as soon as I heard the news. Neither Brian nor Daisy seemed made for such grief. Daisy was nothing like the elegant salesgirl she had been, all she did was yelp at Brian, who sat knocking back shots of whiskey one after another. At each corner of his mouth a deep, vertical furrow had appeared, like a line that had been scored by a firm, resolute, cruel hand.

That was when I started going back to Brooklyn. Brian and I would walk over to Prospect Park, like we used to. He would recount in detail Operation Overlord, in which his son's life had been taken. He had managed, by cross-checking all the information he could get hold of, to pinpoint Harry's death as having taken place near Vierville-sur-Mer during the second wave of the landings, a little before eight in the morning, alongside his comrades from the 16th Infantry Regiment. Brian spent most of his free time studying the course of that day's military operations, and he dreamed that he might one day go there, to Normandy, to stand in the field of white crosses lined up in the green grass, not far from the ocean, and see with his own eyes what Harry would have seen before his young life was cut short. He kept repeating how his son had *died for freedom*, how *proud he was*, that was the expression he used, repeating it as though it were a magic spell that might quell his pain. He spent long hours staring at the photograph of the smiling young GI propped up on the sideboard. I'd known

Harry a little; I remembered him as a happy-go-lucky infant, then a young man with a direct expression and a firm handshake. One might have described him as a young man who didn't yet have a history, his fledgling adult life lived between his bedroom at his parents' house cluttered with sporting trophies, excursions with friends for beer and hamburgers, and occasional jaunts with some young lady named Lucy or Rosie. And then one day he received his draft papers, and it was goodbye to all that. He was not yet twenty-five.

"We're so proud of you, my boy. Don't forget to write. Think of your mother."

"I promise, pops."

And the day of the send-off arrived, though no one knew that it was their final farewell. Brian and Daisy invited me to join them, perhaps out of friendship, or maybe so they wouldn't waver, all alone with him. Brian overdid it a little—*Now you're a man, my son*—while Daisy, with that terrible intuition women have when it comes to their own flesh and blood and the tears they will shed, tried to keep smiling with a courage that I couldn't help but admire.

I remember fixing my eyes on her dangling, colored-glass earrings—too bright, too cheerful—as they swung back and forth like hollow reminders of bygone happiness that would never return. In a few hours, this woman who sold fashionable clothes, all blowsy elegance and commonplace manners, had become a grief-stricken mother, trying to keep a brave face while inside she must have felt torn to pieces. She moved me that day, and when I think back to those difficult hours, I am only too aware that this was the last time she saw her son before he was blown to pieces by German gunners on a beach the other side of the world one beautiful June morning, his life ended just like those of thousands of others who had gone off to fight in a war they knew so little about.

Harry was jolly and serious all at once, aware that this was a moment we would all remember for a long time, that in difficult moments we would have these images to hold on to, until we arrived at some unforeseeable future. We crossed our fingers that the joy of return wouldn't be long in coming and when it arrived it would dilute the intense colors of these memories, privileging what was tangible, flesh and life. From time to time Brian would place his stubby-fingered hand on Daisy's, whenever he felt his courage about to fail him, afraid he would be overwhelmed by a violent, uncontrollable wave of emotion.

I played my role of the family friend, uncle, or kindly godfather, responsible for keeping the conversation going, as you might keep poking a fire that's threatening to go out. Bright sunshine filtered through the gauzy drapes in the fancy Brooklyn restaurant where Brian had chosen to celebrate the departure of his only son. Harry was quite unaccustomed to such extravagance, the profusion of starched tablecloths, glasses, crockery, and silverware whose purpose he could only guess; lips pursed in an appreciative half-smile, he appraised this concrete manifestation of the love and pride of which he had been both object and subject since the day he was born.

I discovered, in this brief, shared moment, the strength and depths of a bond I had not been fully aware of. Suddenly I was overwhelmed by an unbearably precise memory of Liz; I could have sworn she was with us at the table, with her gentle reserve and graceful manners. Had it not been for the dress she wore, which attested to a time of my life that was long past, I would almost have believed I could touch her, that I could smell the faint scent of the eau de toilette she used to dab on her neck every morning after she had fixed her hair. I blinked, gulped down a glass of cold water, and forced myself to turn back to the conversation from which I had briefly drifted away. No one had noticed a thing: for a long time now Liz had existed only in the depths of my heart, the way the light of a star that died billions of years ago remains visible, illuminating the very darkest hours of the night.

Harry's death destroyed Brian, and I had no idea what to say to him, for really there was nothing to say. Time does not heal. After a few days spent with him, trying in vain to offer him some solace, I returned to Ellis Island in a state of deep despondency.

I have one particular memory from this time, of the island being turned into a field of operations, a training camp for the Coast Guard, involving the compulsory reorganization of both the site and its authority, which had to be defended against the officers who had come to train their troops and test new combat equipment. An intrusion I was obliged simultaneously to comply with and to oversee, like being forced to defile a sacred space.

The whistles, the yells of the officers, the sound of helicopters whirring in and out all day long as they unloaded or picked up men and equipment, the navy ships moored right up against the piers—it was all just sound and fury. Like a rehearsal, it was a simulacrum of a war that was taking place elsewhere. Eventually the commotion abated. The army found other locations that were easier to access, where they could be wholly responsible for combat simulations and training elite troops. It took months to rid Ellis of the carcasses of vehicles and the military remains scattered over the island.

At the end of the war, some seven thousand Italians, Germans, and Japanese were jailed at Ellis Island, awaiting deportation. Now I was prison superintendent and warden. I hated that time. I can still recall their shaved skulls and heavy jawlines, our brutal, curt, minimal interactions. The geography of the site changed, the way the different areas were used and organized. There were more metal gates, double doors and locks, new ways to circulate, corridors whose purpose was to maintain isolation. Overseeing this surveillance system was my sole contribution to the world war that was at last coming to an end, my only connection with what was happening in the outside world.

From my vantage point on Ellis Island, I observed the continuing existence of America. The city, so near, so far away. For me, the island had become an outpost, a watchtower or rampart, with me standing sentinel against invasion.

The activity of the station was in inexorable decline. Today I am the captain of a phantom ship that has been abandoned to its ghosts. Like the ghost of Nella, who arrived on board the cursed *Cincinnati* on April 23, 1923, and still clamors for justice today.

ELLIS ISLAND, NOVEMBER 6,
5 O'CLOCK IN THE MORNING.

A steamship arriving in the bay was visible at first as no more than a dot on the horizon; gradually it grew to the size of a box of matches, its silhouette becoming more detailed with every second: the line of its three red funnels, the acute angle of the bow, and the long black surface of the hull, topped by a pierced white bulkhead composed of bridges, bulwarks, and portholes. It would sail right past Ellis Island without stopping, as though we didn't even exist at that point, even though we already knew its name, where it had come from, and how many passengers were on board.

Those who worked at Ellis Island saw

these steamships simply as an assignment, a quantity of individuals to be disembarked and distributed as quickly as possible to undergo a multitude of mysterious procedures, but I was struck every time by the sight of the newcomers, the knots of people massed on the bridges waving at the promised land, and by the silent majesty of the massive structure that had just crossed the ocean. I was always moved at the thought of all these people who had risked their lives on board for a fate as yet unknown.

After the swift disembarkation at New York Harbor of the first- and second-class passengers, the passengers in steerage were transferred to a barge and brought here for the rite of passage they all dreaded.

The April morning of the *Cincinnati*'s arrival was bright and frosty, after a bitterly cold, snowy winter. The days were growing longer and the sky was clear, cloudless, unmenacing. It was just another chilly spring day. As usual, the passengers carried their possessions off with them, hurried along by the personnel in charge of their orientation. *Hurry up, hurry up, this way, quickly, no, you can't sit down, keep moving, keep moving.* As soon as they arrived in the Great Hall they were told to deposit their belongings, which they did most unwillingly, with desperate tears and much suspicion and protest, despite assurances that everything would be waiting for them where they had left it. It was all they still had of their previous lives—usually little more than some worn linen and modest toiletries, a few pictures, a violin or a harmonica, a Bible, a cross, a menorah, or a painted icon—after the distress of leaving almost all they owned behind were they to add the loss of the last of their meager possessions?

Most had no idea what awaited them here, despite having received letters from those who had already made it, or having heard tales of it round and about. They had nothing to shield them from the ordeal they faced. For most it would last only a few hours, for some it might be days, a few would be denied entry and sent back. In spite of the small number of those who were turned away—according to my statistics no more than two percent—the fear that they might find themselves among the deportees caused them unspeakable anguish.

That morning, it was a group of Italian passengers from the *Cincinnati* who were following in the footsteps of those who had come before.

I happened to be approaching the staircase where the initial selection took place; I had been summoned in the morning by a team of construction workers to give my opinion on some work in progress and to discuss the need to increase the perimeter of a works area. This summed up my daily life, for the most part. I was being asked to purchase more materials, and I wanted to see what was going on for myself. I was on my way back to my office to give instructions for ordering supplies when I heard shrieking from the top of the stairs. This was not unusual here, and in general I thought myself immune to such sounds, but the howls of distress I heard froze my blood. A young Italian woman in a long black skirt and white blouse, locks of dark hair poking out from her headscarf, seemed to be beseeching the medical officers who stood facing her. I couldn't stop myself moving discreetly closer to observe the scene. It didn't take me long to figure out what was going on. She was refusing to let go of the hand of a tall, sturdily built boy who looked about fifteen. She was clearly too young to be his mother. His sister, I supposed. Chalked on the boy's gray coat I saw the fateful sign: the letter X with a circle around it: clear evidence of mental deficiency. Not even a plain X, "suspected," offering the benefit of the doubt.

A person thus identified would be isolated before undergoing additional tests and examinations, though this rarely led to a change of diagnosis. Deportation to his country of origin by the next steamship, at the expense of the shipping company. The line doctors had guessed right, it seemed to me. The boy looked from one doctor to the other with a frightened expression, and, despite his height and build, he cowered like a child by the young woman's side. He didn't utter a word. An interpreter explained to the young woman that this was the procedure; the boy had to go with them to another area to await the final decision. He had to undergo further tests, and she was not allowed to stay with him; she had to sit on a bench and wait. Her own situation seemed in order; she would be called over when her turn came to answer the standard questionnaire. If everything was as it should be, she would be allowed to leave the island and would be in Manhattan in a few hours.

Over time, Italian had become the foreign language I understood best and I had ended up being able to speak it, I'm not sure how. Alongside the jarring sound of many Slavic languages, it seemed almost easy, and my relative facility permitted me to communicate and to skim through letters and documents when necessary.

The young woman was trying to explain that he was an innocent, steady, hardworking boy who posed no problem to anyone, and that she could not possibly leave his side. No word, nothing anybody said, could calm the young woman down, and the moment the boy was unceremoniously led away from her he uttered a frightening, guttural, barely human cry. She collapsed in hysterical tears and was led—almost carried—by two officers who sat her down in an empty place by the wall on one of the benches in the last row. She was out of sight of most of the other passengers, the only Italian near a group of impatient and garrulous Ukrainian Jews in black caftans and hats who paid her no attention whatsoever.

She was underdressed for the season, with only a shawl over her blouse, and, desperately scared, she was both shivering and trembling. I was overcome with immense pity. It was awful to witness her suffering. I had time to observe her, her olive complexion and green eyes, her strong, knotted hands that looked as though they had aged faster than her face, her lean, sinewy, nervous physique. I went to fetch one of the thin gray blankets that we gave out to people who were to spend a night or more here. I came back, and, without saying anything, I draped the fabric over her shoulders.

With this gesture, I crossed the invisible line over which there is no possible return. She flinched as she felt the material on her shoulders, then tried to wrap herself in it, casting me a questioning glance. Who was I? What did I want from her? Should she get up and follow me? Was this normal? Was there news about her brother? I saw all these questions in her eyes. It seemed as though nobody saw or heard her; I have never felt such a sense of loneliness and distress, and I did something I had never done before, and should not have done then, but I know I would have killed anyone who tried to stop me. I sat down next to her and, though I already knew the answer, I asked what her name was and to explain to me what was going on.

Calmer now, she sat up straight and wiped her face. She told me that her name was Nella Casarini and that she was from Sardinia. She had done the crossing with her younger brother Paolo, who was all the family she had, and they could never be separated. *La supplico, signore.* She repeated what she had said earlier at the top of the stairs, what the interpreter had repeated to the medical officers: Paolo was just a boy, a bit simple, but hardworking and gentle, he needed her, he was unable to look after himself. *Sono la sua sorella, sua madre.* I am his sister, his mother. I cannot leave him. America is our last chance. We have nothing, nowhere else to go.

I listened attentively, concentrating on what she said. We were no longer in the Great Hall filled with rows of benches and surrounded by hundreds of indifferent passengers, all too immersed in their own lives to take any interest in the drama of a neighbor of whose language and origins they knew nothing. I was no longer the commissioner, a uniformed officer of the Federal Immigration Service, and she was no longer an anonymous immigrant, desperate and stricken with fear. At that moment, all the attention I was paying her turned into something terrible, violent, and uncontrollable. I desired her.

This was a clinical statement based on spontaneous evidence. All those years, every single day I had crossed paths with women of all ages. They were either employees under my authority, and I could not consider them otherwise, or immigrants, from different worlds, worlds I would never know, my only concern for whom was their compatibility with a future American citizenship. Sometimes at night the sexual urge would encroach, insistent and agonizing, demanding a relief that left me in a state of melancholy and loathing that I came to dread more and more each time. It was not as though this lost, shivering young woman possessed a single one of the attributes that normally inspires fantasies in a man, yet I had to admit that she provoked in me a desire mixed with compassion that frightened me. I hastened back to my office and buried myself in a thousand tasks in a futile attempt to distract my thoughts. A short while later I returned to the Great Hall, where she was still sitting on the bench, her face in her hands, as if she were trying to block out all sight of her surroundings. Perhaps she was praying.

I could not justify spending more time with her, it was not my place, even though I was not obliged to justify my presence here or anywhere in the station—I was, after all, the commissioner, but that would not prevent embarrassing rumors circulating. I bade her farewell with some hackneyed platitudes, assuring her we would do everything we could to resolve her and her brother's situation with the utmost fairness. It was all bunk, of course. I would have loved to believe those warm words, so far from what I really wanted to say to her, but it was obvious from first sight that her brother's case was already decided. A little later I went to check that she was comfortably settled. She had been served a hot meal that she hadn't touched. I requested the daily report from the health inspectors. It was hopeless, of course. I felt the walls of my office closing in, suffocating me. I already knew that my violent desire, mixed with a disconcerting compassion, would lead me very far away from the man I thought I was. I also understood that no reasoning was going to make me turn back. I did not sleep that night.

I remember how cold the apartment was. It was the in-between season, unsettled, reluctant to renounce the temperature that had set in, and despite the approaching new season's signs of impatience, the weather was vacillating between sluggish winter and faltering spring. I turned on the heater that Liz often used at this time of year, and tried to lose myself in a book as a way to erase from my thoughts the images that had taken over my mind and my body.

This young, dark-haired, distraught Italian woman had somehow touched an unknown region in me, a part of me whose existence I had never suspected, the sudden discovery of which was like being handed a mirror and seeing a stranger in its reflection. I determined to spend the next day finding out more about her.

Added to this decision was the need to

act with discretion; I believed myself up until that point to have exercised my responsibilities with integrity, and I had no desire for my reputation to be destroyed in a matter of hours. Nella saw me as I walked past the dormitory the next morning. She gave me the very faintest smile, her eyes revealing that she recognized me, and the feverish expectation I read there sent a tremor through me.

Under the pretext that I needed to examine the cases of some of the *Cincinnati*'s passengers, I asked that a few, including Nella, be brought to my office to be interviewed. I dispatched the other wretched souls with a few pointless questions, whose answers were of no interest to me, and at last found myself alone with Nella. I was pleased that I understood enough of her language to be able to do without Luigi Chianese, the station's principal Italian interpreter, whose shifty, obsequious demeanor irritated me to the point that I preferred to do without his services whenever I could. Rather than staying behind my desk, I came and sat down beside Nella. Intimidated, she sat stiff and upright on her chair, nervously smoothing the worn fabric of her skirt. I began mentally to assemble all the things I had learned about her since the previous day, as one might piece together a photograph ripped from a newspaper to try and guess the elements that are missing. I didn't hide from Nella the difficulty of her case, and could only promise that she would be allowed to see her brother and that I would look into all the possible solutions, then I recalled Paolo's guileless, frightened expression and was ashamed of my words. I sensed that she was torn between her fear of saying something that would doom them forever, and her desire to open up to me, to unbosom herself of the details of her difficult life.

I listened, then came the moment I had imagined a hundred times since the previous night. I put out my hand and placed it on hers. I had the presence of mind to ask my secretaries in the office neighboring mine to stop what they were doing and devote themselves to digging up an imaginary folder that supposedly dealt with some members of Nella's family who had arrived a few years back. I returned to my office. She hadn't moved. I saw her tuck a lock of hair behind her ear; there was such simplicity and grace in the gesture that it took my breath away. I took her hand again and helped her up. She was quite tall, taller than I had realized, and she stood facing me with a strange mixture of reserve and acquiescence, restraint and abandon. I approached closer still and took her in my arms, awkwardly, a movement that was like a foreign language to me now. And then tears, her tears, burning, abundant, endless. I thought of her anguish, her fatigue, the discovery of so many unfamiliar things at once, her unbearable wait. And my desire for her, for all of her, the need to feel her sinewy, dark hands on my body, and within this desire, a yearning to soothe her troubles and to spare her any more.

I forced myself to do something to bring this feverish, tense moment to an end. Any second a colleague might come to the door, and such an unusual interview, so lengthy and without any witnesses, would certainly give rise to suspicion, insinuation, and instantaneous rumormongering. I called a member of staff to accompany Nella and, intent on being as visible as possible, summoned an inspector on some pretext invented just a few moments before. I needed to be alone to think straight, to relive each minute spent with Nella, and I was afraid, horribly afraid, to find myself entertaining such disturbing feelings. I worked late that night, or rather I left my office at a late hour to return to my apartment. Between these two enclosed spaces, these two places of silence, I could hear the incessant commotion of life at Ellis Island, frenzied and hectic, echoing and indistinct. Even more than usual, I had the impression of being on the open seas, on a ship being steered carefully and with prudence, before which all of a sudden a terrifying iceberg loomed whose dangerous proximity defied any maneuver. That night, like the previous one, I took a long time to fall asleep.

The next day I was completely taken up with quotidian tasks, in addition to which I requested immediate updates on the status of all passengers who were being held here, including the group from the *Cincinnati*. Of course I learned nothing new, and the emergency of the day was the arrival of some Irish passengers who came off the boat in an indescribable state. Ridden with lice and bedbugs, with cockroaches running around in their luggage, covered in scabies, infested with pellagra, they were sent straight to quarantine and all their belongings to be disinfected. Report; statement to the shipping company; cross-examination of the ship's officials; overflowing infirmary; distribution of clean linen. We also had to deal with the cries of the women and the silent hostility of the men who had to be shaved and who felt humiliated with their naked skulls, blue-tinged skin, and protruding bones. This was the usual stuff of my daily life but I desperately wanted to be elsewhere. Nonetheless, after everyone had received their orders, like a crew preparing to meet an attack from an enemy ship, the situation eventually calmed down somewhat. Whether it was the calm after the battle, or before the storm, I could not say.

I suppose that in spite of the extra work, in spite of the nervous tension that resulted from it, a secret voice continued to flow through me without my being aware of it. I found another excuse to have Nella brought to my office. She looked as nervous and reserved as ever, seemed to be trying to understand the rules and laws that governed this place, so far removed from anything she knew, and she thanked me for allowing her to see and speak to her brother.

A silence arose between us, and then an odd thing happened, one of those incidents that only lasts a moment, but the memory of which haunts you forever. There was a strange noise outside the window of my office. A thump against the glass, followed by a sort of crumpling. We both started and looked up at the same time, and I realize that this was probably the only time we ever both had the same instinctive reaction. A large gray seagull had flown into the window and was trying to regain its balance, furiously flapping its wings. Then it stopped moving and leaned against the window for a long time, quite still, apparently observing us with one black, piercing eye. I had never seen such a thing before. Nella recoiled, terrified. I saw her making several signs of the cross in quick succession and uttering some words that I did not grasp. The seagull did not move. Nella stared at it, fear written all over her face, and then looked at me without saying anything. I felt cleaved in two by her expression.

To put an end to the unbearable tension, I took a step towards her and seized her hands. I drew her to me and held her there for a long time, without saying a word, as if the warmth of her body alone was going to help me recover a lost world. She stepped away from me and seemed to grow calm, or perhaps I wanted to convince myself she had.

I noticed that she was wearing a different blouse, made of finer fabric, with a lace trim at the neck and wrist. Was this modest attempt at elegance meant for me? I rather suspected in fact that she had decided to present herself in her finest clothes in honor of an interview whose import she did not know, but which she sensed was of decisive importance. Like the previous day, her eyes expressed an intense expectation and a silent supplication. Without knowing what I was about to say, I heard myself offer her my help. In what way, I had no idea yet. Would I have bribed one of the physicians, or used my authority to obtain an exemption? Might I have written and initialed an exit permit from Ellis Island and a certificate of citizenship? I could not have said at that moment what I was prepared to do to help her. All I would have been able to say was that I was determined to do something. In a few inexplicable seconds I was ready to do anything. I had already entered dangerous and uncertain territory, but it was all just beginning.

Had I ever desired a woman as much as

Nella Casarini? I think not. My body in torment, my mind in confusion, I suggested that I meet her after dinner at the entrance to the dormitory. My eyes remained fixed on hers, and I suddenly felt the muscles in her arm relax, as though in surrender. *D'accordo?* She looked back at me in silence and then lowered her head, apparently lost in observation of the folds of her skirt. I was in a daze, confused, faraway. The world around me no longer existed, all that mattered was what I had decided to go through with later that night. In those hours, the distinction between what was good, evil, lawful, or forbidden had no meaning for me. In a few minutes Nella had taken possession of my whole world.

The dining room held more than a thousand people; it was an immense space furnished with tables and benches, with a strong smell of cooking, and a great din of flatware and heavy, white earthenware plates. I looked for her in the throng, without success. Where was she? I was reassured when I found her waiting for me at the entrance to the dormitory. She seemed even leaner, her skin even darker; she still had the blanket over her shoulders that she had tried to tie like a shawl. Around her, men, women, and children were going in and out. Nobody paid us any attention. I gestured for her to follow me down the corridor that led to my rooms. When we reached the doorway she stopped still. I took her hand and drew her inside. I sensed her freeze when she saw the bed. I stepped closer to her, caressed her face, and began to remove her clothes. I tried to be as gentle as I could, in spite of the mounting desire that made me oblivious to everything else, but my movements were clumsy and rushed. She was still and silent, and remained so when I took her, rougher and faster than I had wanted. She stifled a cry of pain, I ejaculated, and it was over. As I drew away, I saw the sheet was stained with blood. Nella Casarini had never known a man before.

I made a tentative, gentle gesture, looking away as she stood up. I pointed towards the bathroom where I had laid out a clean towel for her. There was hope in her eyes, an immense, terrifying hope. A few hours later, I accompanied her back to the dormitory. I was in love, madly in love with Nella Casarini, troubled by what she had told me about her life, and prepared to do anything for her, prepared to try anything and to deny everything.

I barely slept again that night, and arrived at my office early the next morning, every possible solution going round and round in my head. What if I were to marry her? This idea, which presented itself unexpectedly, like a butterfly in flight, was transformed in a few minutes into a solution. The solution. The only solution, in no way betraying the memory of my beloved Liz. Nella was the only woman I had even glanced at since the terrible time when Liz had passed away. The only woman who had revived, without even trying to, the desire for love that was swelling inside me. I was ashamed of my haste, of my hurried and clumsy movements, but I had the rest of my life ahead of me to repair it.

As I sat lost in thought, two night wardens came into my office with grim expressions on their faces. *Sir, there's been an accident. We found the body of the Italian boy, the idiot. He threw himself from a window on the top floor. We've cleaned up the body and put it in the machinery shed. What do we do now?* I felt faint. I couldn't tell if this was real life or if I was dreaming. *Sir, should we wake the interpreter to inform the family? No point disturbing the doctor, there's no emergency.* I was struggling to breathe. Answers, I had to provide answers, take the usual measures, initiate the procedures to be followed in such circumstances. I pretended I had something I needed to deal with first. I needed to be alone for a few minutes.

It wasn't to be. News travels fast on this sloop. Before I had even called for him, and despite my reluctance to use his services, Luigi Chianese, clean-shaven, neatly dressed, and as obsequious as ever, was at the door, already aware of the situation without having been informed.

He was a strange man, this Chianese. Watchful, prickly, irascible. In spite of his mood swings and his unpredictable behavior, he had made himself indispensable with his command of half a dozen languages, inherited from his Polish mother and Italian father. Born from this surprising union, he had an incessant desire to rise above the tasks entrusted to him. Ambitious and hardworking, he spent his evenings studying law, and I later discovered, when he announced his departure from the station, that he had gotten his law degree and was joining a large Manhattan firm. I presumed that he was entering through the back door and would be dealing with minor traffic offenses and straightforward divorces for modest and irregular fees. The kind of client who doesn't always pay up and the kind of work that is overwhelmingly dull. He was bound to find his place.

I learned later that he had become a highly sought-after lawyer, renowned for both his single-mindedness and his interpersonal skills. Truth be told I was not altogether surprised; it was justice, after all. At Ellis Island, I had appreciated his talents, but I had never trusted him. I hated the way he had of interfering in matters that were not of his concern, and of making them more complicated than they were. More than once, I had to summon him to my office to insist that he stick to exercising the skills for which he had been employed. Each time, I told myself that he was the kind of man to whom you should never give an inch or turn your back.

He stood facing me, his hair slicked back and parted precisely down the middle, with the bow tie he always wore in an attempt to appear elegant or rakish that seemed to me to be quite out of place on Ellis Island. *I heard the news, sir. Tell me what I can do.* Things were happening now over which I had no control; I just had to follow without being overwhelmed by events. First, for the sake of form, I had to have the body identified—a terribly sad sight—and register the death with a doctor.

We went to the dormitory next. Nella was already dressed and sitting, hands on knees, on her cot. That acrid nighttime odor of confinement, unwashed bodies, and sweat, in the white light of the morning. I looked at her with pity, silhouetted against the bed in her long black skirt. She lifted her eyes to us questioningly. I gestured to Luigi Chianese—he was already in character, like an actor waiting impatiently in the wings, quivering with excitement—to be silent, and then I spoke. I closed my eyes for a moment. I had barely uttered a few words when I heard a bestial howl, a dreadful cry that seemed to come from somewhere in her gut. She collapsed onto the cot. I went towards her, not really knowing what I wanted to do. I tried what I hoped was a comforting gesture, but there was nothing to comfort. She screamed and screamed, her body convulsing with fear, pain, panic, and despair. A group of Italians drew near, their faces pale with shock. They stood around her, not daring to speak or touch her. I learned later that they, too, were passengers from the *Cincinnati* who had also been retained here for various reasons. It was not until later, much later, that I heard the strange tale that bound them all to one another.

Nella then seemed to unfold, taut as a bow, and stood to face me. She had stopped crying. She addressed me, her voice hoarse, suddenly transformed, her hand outstretched. The interpreter tried to intervene but I stopped him and asked him to go and leave me to deal with the situation. The Italians drew closer, glaring at me with animosity. Nella began to speak, her eyes never leaving my face. Her voice, low and steady, seemed not to belong to her, as if her words came from somewhere far away and she was merely the conduit. She shouted, raising her arms in an imprecation to heaven. She was transformed into a howl of rage, of revolt. *Maledetto, morire, acqua e fuoco!* She cursed me, vowing that I would die by fire and water.

Then there was a long silence. Her body buckled, seeming to shrink inside her skirt, she took her face in her hands and shook with sobs. Two women kept me away from her by forming a barrier between us with their bodies and skirts. I muttered a few awkward things that no one heard, perhaps I didn't actually say them out loud, and then quickly left the room without another word.

I went back to my office to complete the official procedures in the event of suicide; it was not the first to take place here. All the steps had to be followed rigorously, and I needed to produce a report immediately. In view of the horrible state of the body, the unfortunate boy was buried the following afternoon in the presence of his sister and a handful of their compatriots whom fate had thrown together. There was singing, women's voices to send shivers down the spine, prayers, ululation, tears. Nella remained walled up in her silence. Using the pretext of an imminent extension to the cemetery, I had the grave dug a little away from others. The next day Nella left for Manhattan with the rest of the Italians from the *Cincinnati*, apart from one, Francesco Lazzarini, with whom I was to have many dealings in the weeks that followed, for a variety of reasons. It was thanks to him—whatever this confession costs me—that I gained some keys to understanding Nella. Keys that were not of course meant to open any doors, but merely to allow me a glimpse of a horrifying tale.

Welcome to America. What happened to Nella Casarini? In spite of all my best efforts, I never learned her fate, a fact that has become more and more difficult to bear. It was an era when anything was possible. All my searches came to nothing, then one day I thought I had found her. Thinking back to that moment, as I have done so often, I am convinced it was her—the woman I spotted a few years after the tragedy one summer's day on a bench in Manhattan—and not a mere effect of my disturbed imagination. How hard it is for me to admit! Perhaps later. I have tried to forget her fury against me, however legitimate it was. So many years have passed. Nothing has changed.

ELLIS ISLAND, NOVEMBER 7,
6 O'CLOCK IN THE MORNING.

During the days that followed Nella Casarini's departure, I forced myself to make the greatest effort to continue working and behaving with a semblance of normality. I felt as though I had locked myself away, somewhere deep inside myself, completely indifferent to the rest of the world. I spoke only the few words necessary to get through the day without raising suspicions. One question haunted me: who had told him, who had made the unfortunate boy comprehend the reality of the fate that awaited him? Had he overheard it? Somewhere in his poor, messed-up head he had understood that his separation from Nella was forever, and decided it would be better to die. How could he have guessed that I had decided to marry Nella and that, with her new status, he would be given permission to stay with his sister? Of course he couldn't have known, it was impossible. Perhaps he had fathomed what was going to happen, that his separation from Nella upon their arrival was definitive, and perhaps despite his inability to understand properly what was going on he recognized intuitively, viscerally, something that was impossible to accept.

Strange as it may seem, no one made any allusion to what had happened, not even Luigi Chianese, whose indiscretion and gossiping I dreaded. It must be said that the frequency of such incidents was unfortunately high, and I, like the rest of the station staff, had ended up, if not trivializing them, at least accepting them with a certain fatalism, as the necessary price to pay for access to the Promised Land. Sacrifices were needed, a few expiatory victims to offer up to Moloch. This was how it was and it had to be accepted. America, for all her generosity, could not accommodate anyone who was a burden or a potential danger. Newcomers tried their luck at their own risk, and for the people dealing with them, the daily workload was so heavy it left little time for any emotion. For me, the story was different. The guilty memory of the hours I had spent with Nella, the knowledge that I had forced her to give herself up to me, competed with the intense memory of her taut, lean body, her skin, her hair, her thighs. My nights are interminable now.

That night we spent together, before she returned along the cold, dimly lit corridors to the dormitory, Nella told me a little about her life. I encouraged her with a few questions, curious to know who she was, where she came from, intrigued by the presence of such a young woman, alone with and responsible for her feeble-minded brother. I was curious about her strong body, her hands, tanned and calloused from what I suspected was hard, physical toil. If I were to help her, I had to at least try and understand her situation. The story Nella told me, interspersed with long silences and hesitations, was strange; I would never have imagined crossing paths with someone who had lived such a life. Now all I have left are memories, but those hours during which she confided in me, guardedly, torn between the fear of confessing something that would promptly condemn her and the need to share her harrowing experiences, remain imprinted on my memory with dreadful precision. Her black hair was spread over the white sheets as she sought to cover her bare shoulders, the rest of her body hidden beneath the covers, tracing a sinuous line down the center of my bed. And her voice, her low voice in the darkness, recounting her startling story. And I, trying to follow as best I could. And my desire for her, rising again.

Over time, through nights and years of sleeplessness, I have tried to reconstruct her story. I endeavored to do this based on what she told me, adding to it things that Lazzarini later told me, and a few details tossed out by Chianese, based on information he extorted from some of the *Cincinnati* passengers, whose trust he played on because of their shared mother tongue, which he undoubtedly used to convince them that he had more power on Ellis Island than he actually did.

All these different voices, all these elements related—or in some cases perhaps invented—by one person or another, helped me piece together Nella's story in a way I wanted to understand it. But I wouldn't be being completely honest if I neglected to

admit that my own imagination sometimes served as a link, a bridge, between
details that were missing, fragmentary, or
unclear.

Nella was only nineteen years old. She
was born in Sardinia, the poorest of the
poor, in an isolated house outside the hamlet of Sozza, near the village of Padru, surrounded by mountains, wind, and barren
land. She lived with her father, Giuseppe,
and her brother Paolo. She looked after the
house, watched over her brother, and prepared her father's meals. They had a few
animals that gave milk and meat—chick-
ens, sheep, and goats—some olive and fig
trees, and nothing else. They saw no one
and the world stopped at the edge of their
fields. Nella's father was not like other men.
He kept his distance, and when he went to
Sozza, or more rarely to Padru, the villagers went out of their way to avoid him, and
for nothing in the world would they look
him in the eye. They would hurry past,
their fingers crossed behind their backs,
and hastily recite an Ave Maria or a prayer
to the holy protector. As far as everyone

was concerned, Giuseppe Casarini was a *jettatore*, a caster of spells, who could make entire herds die, rot or shrivel any meager hopes for a harvest, cause the water in the spring to run dry, make women infertile and husbands impotent. He was the evil eye. Whatever he looked at was cursed, doomed to misfortune or destruction; he knew the devil's incantations for bringing down misery on the world, and his off-spring were no better than him: a feral daughter who spoke to no one, and a simpleton built like a bear, who followed her around like a shadow.

From birth, Paolo was not like other children. He was late to walk and to talk, and when he did talk he said little. When Giuseppe's wife died of a bad cough one damp winter, he was unable to cope, and it was Nella, who was only a few years old, who took care of her brother, protecting him from their father's impatience and anger. Paolo grew big and strong, but his brain remained feeble. Nella and he invented a secret language, made up of sounds, intonations, and gestures, by which they understood each other. In the evening, Nella would tell him stories, like her mother used to do—"How Saint Anthony Stole Fire from the Devil," or "The Little Calf with the Golden Horns," his favorite. The story he asked his sister to tell him most often would send him, according to Nella, into raptures, soothing the fretfulness that grew more apparent towards nightfall. In those moments, Nella told me with a smile that pierced my heart, *I realized that my poor Paolo's confused head was sometimes shot through with sunshine, and it was because of such moments that I made myself carry on hoping.* How much did Paolo really understand? Was he simply lulled by his sister's gentle voice, in which he could sense the deep calm that signaled the end of the day and the onset of night?

One day Giuseppe decided it was time to pass on his special gifts to his daughter. He taught her to watch out for and interpret signs, how to predict when death was about to strike by distinguishing its message in the voice of the wind, or the howl of a civet, or the way a solitary sparrow perched on the roof of a house, or a barn owl's hooting, or the frayed nerves of a pack of dogs. He taught her the secret significance of a rooster crowing at midnight, and that of a red halo around the moon, heralding blood. He divulged the meaning of a dead hen discovered in the morning, evidence of the passage of the Grim Reaper, who had chosen to attack an animal rather than a human being, but who was prowling the neighborhood and sure to return.

He told her about the cotillion of the dead, the joyous music one sometimes hears when walking past the church at night. The invitation to celebrate with them must be refused, for their only wish is to bear someone away with them, feet not even touching the ground; though they always find one trusting soul, tempted by the promise of wine and dancing, to join them.

When Nella was born, Giuseppe had no intention of passing on his gifts and his wisdom to his daughter. But one morning, when she was still a child, Nella woke up with her body covered in bruises, and he realized that it was a waste of effort to imagine that she was going to return to the common people, for she had been chosen. When he questioned her, Nella told him she had dreamed of a woman from the village who had recently died, and who had asked her to send a message to her family, without which her soul was unable to find rest. Nella was to be the messenger: the family was to make offerings, say prayers, and celebrate mass, and she would be plied with money and gifts for her trouble. Knowing nothing of the spirit world, Nella had not conveyed the message, and the dead soul had made clear her displeasure with a frenzied attack on her. Giuseppe understood immediately, and sent the child, in her cleanest dress, to speak to the bereaved relatives. He told her that she could not escape her ancestral destiny. He showed her the potency of herbs, myrtle, stones, and roots, and the power of prayer. He taught her incantations and spells, gestures that heal and words that cast malign curses. None of this shocked or frightened Nella. And until Giuseppe's death she remained carefree, more afraid of the winter cold, the mistral, the sirocco, and the terrible droughts of summer, than the presence of invisible forces.

Sitting around the fire at night in the village, speaking in low voices so the devil wouldn't hear, people said that Giuseppe's father and grandfather, and all the men before them since time immemorial, were men who'd quit the company of men to run with the wolves and lead the packs. They spoke the language of the beasts, understood the meaning of every twitch, knew how to be accepted by wearing a cloth impregnated with the secretions of a female wolf in heat. The dominant male, and all the others, showed their subservience by the droop of their spines and tails. Many a lost traveler or shepherd returning late to his flock would see him, a tall figure walking at the head of the pack, staff in hand, dressed in the skin of one of the animals; or at nightfall, sitting in a clearing by a flickering fire, surrounded by wolves keeping a respectful distance. Yes, such stories were told in the hamlets around Padru, and even beyond. The wolf leader walked through the village at night, followed by his pack, collecting food and coins left on doorsteps for him by villagers desperate to obtain his protection, or at least his indifference, for they feared reprisals too. Goats and sheep slaughtered, poultry houses destroyed, and other things no one dared to say out loud: sometimes he adopted the appearance of a husband in order to possess the wife, who only realized it too late from the musky smell of his seed, or when she spotted a clawed foot slipping into a boot hastily unlaced in the dark, or when her suspicions were raised by an unexpectedly forceful embrace. The leader was bound to the darkest forces of nature and held absolute sway over the other wolves; everyone knew they licked his hands and formed around him an impenetrable barrier of sharp teeth and untamed flesh.

For generations, no one had ever found the corpse of a wolf leader. It was said that upon the death of a leader the pack would gather in a circle and weep real tears for several days and nights, at the end of which the leader's soul was reborn in the body of one of that year's cubs. Such were the things muttered during vigils in the hamlet, along with many other things as well: it was Giuseppe, and then Nella, who were behind the mysteries. Now the villagers had an unequivocal explanation for the fears that haunted them and the sorrows that beset their hardscrabble lives. For centuries they had sought reasons and explanations, and in the end blaming everything on Giuseppe and Nella must have seemed to them infinitely more reassuring than railing in vain against an unresponsive sky, giving in to their fate without being able to assign responsibility to anyone. They found, in this named and identified duality of Good and Evil, simple answers, an outline of the way the universe is organized that enabled them to accept their hopeless fate with either gratitude or resignation.

One day Giuseppe fell, his foot caught on the branch of a fig tree, or perhaps the branch yielded under his weight. Nobody was present, and the fall was fatal. When Nella mentioned her father's death, I didn't understand what he was doing in the tree, or at what time of year the accident occurred, and I dared not make her relive those hours that inspired in her such terrible fear. She told me that some shepherds from the village found the body. Concerned that her father had not returned home the previous day, Nella learned the news on her way to the village the next morning. Someone spat it out to her face as she turned a corner. The villagers didn't want to return the body to her, or to give him a Christian burial. She saw women bending down to pick up rocks, and advancing towards her threateningly. One of the stones struck her brow; she still had the scar on her temple, like a tiny star. Terrified, she ran home to fetch her brother and, fearing they would be attacked, they hid in the woods outside the village, waiting to see what would become of their father's body.

In the evening they saw a group of ten men leaving the village, among whom she recognized the Cavallari brothers, the tall Pietro and the one-eyed Fabiano; Luca Rossi, the blacksmith; Aldo Mancini, the tinsmith; and Sandro Morelli, the son of the innkeeper, led by Don Simone, the priest. A donkey pulled a cart in which they could see a long figure wrapped in a sheet. Don Simone, in his short, grubby cassock, walked ahead, brandishing above his head the processional crucifix. Nella had always been afraid of him, of his sunken eyes, his hooked nose, his thundering voice that seemed capable only of retribution and contempt. From their hiding place, Nella and her brother watched the strange, ominous procession making its way into the forest, where the men eventually halted. Don Simone seemed to be leading the operation. The men lifted the body and laid it in a large ditch between two rocks. Then they covered it with stones, large and small, to make a heavy mound. Nobody was going to come and pray at this grave; its very existence would be forgotten. No one would know that Giuseppe the *jettatore* had ever even existed.

The two children watched the scene in silence, Nella clutching her brother to her, terrified that a cry, a sob, or a sudden movement would betray them. The men finished their work and began making their way back to the village. The children waited a while then emerged from their hiding place and began following the road home through the hills. Approaching the house, they had a view of it down below. The men had reached it before them. The Cavallaris, Rossis, Mancinis, Morellis, and all the others, except Don Simone. They were waiting with pitchforks and sticks. Nella was sure that her heart was about to stop beating and she hugged Paolo to her as tightly as she could; he was hungry, he wanted to go home. He began to whimper. Nella knew only too well the fate that awaited her. Two years earlier, the Cavallari brothers, the tall one and the one-eyed one, had forced a girl from the village of Monti into a barn after a dance. The next day, the young woman threw herself into a well. The villagers found her gold cross and chain and her shoes neatly lined up alongside it.

Nella and Paolo stood there, paralyzed with fear, not knowing what to do. Night had fallen, but Nella could still see the pale splashes of the men's shirts as they circled the house. They would stop to speak to one another, then wander off to beat at the nearest bushes, then come together again in a strange, disturbing ballet. When she saw sparks crackling in the darkness she stifled a cry. Then came real flames, swiftly followed by a huge conflagration. Nella and Paolo had nothing left, only their lives and the clothes they stood up in. They had no choice but to flee.

That night, they walked the eighteen kilometers that separated them from the port of Olbia. In the morning, they stole something to eat and spent the day at the harbor watching the boats. In the evening, they managed to stow away in the hold of a boat that plied the route to Naples. Dirty and hungry, they waited a long time before they were able to get off the *Veloce* without being seen. Now they had to find a way to scrape a living. Nella found work serving food and washing dishes at a bar in the harbor, and Paolo carried crates and containers of merchandise to the docks. Above their heads, the blue of the sky; in front of their eyes, the Bay of Naples; and in the distance the sinuous outline of Vesuvius dissolving in the mist. They slept huddled on a straw mattress provided to Nella in an attic room over the bar. They had escaped the worst. Whatever happened tomorrow, fate could only smile on them now.

MIDDAY.

In Naples, Nella was constantly dodging men's hands, glances, obscene gestures, and crude jokes; she made sure to avoid dark passages and alleyways. It was only in the evening, when Paolo came home exhausted from carrying crates as heavy as he, that Nella felt safe, that her world was whole again. It was in the bar that she first heard talk of America. In her eyes, Naples represented the limits of the known world, and the existence of other continents, other oceans, was no less foreign to her than that of the stars or other planets.

At every table the conversation revolved around *La Merica*—those who had left, those who were planning to leave, letters received or awaited, the dreams of those who remained. *La Merica* was the celestial Jerusalem, the land of Canaan, the temple of Solomon, the hanging gardens of Babylon, and the certainty of never going hungry again. The whole of Italy was dreaming of America. The tales of those who had already taken the step, or rather the ocean, became fragments or snatches of a saga that transformed them into intrepid heroes, thanks to the determination they had shown to reverse the course of their wretched lives.

They were the conquistadors, the victors, and their words helped construct a hallowed myth. Letters home, which sometimes took up to two months to arrive, bore colorful US stamps. Mail was tangible proof of the existence of a world on the other side of the ocean. Much more than private correspondence containing personal news, the purpose of these letters was to prove to those who had stayed behind that their relatives had found success; they were read aloud in people's homes, in cafés and in bars, and the news they contained was circulated and discussed at every opportunity. Gino's son had seen with his own eyes streets that were paved with gold; Luca and Maria had just had a third son whom they named John; Pietro, a laborer from Sampieri, cultivated vegetables the size of a small child, a few of which would be sufficient to feed the entire village. Every day at the bar Nella heard stories like this that made men's eyes shine, filled fathers with pride.

Stay or leave. They had to choose between the cast-iron certainty of poverty and the possibility of a future as prodigious as it was miraculous. It was either staying with their compatriots on their ancestral land, land that had belonged to the generations that preceded them, or being prepared to leave behind everything of their present lives. Sometimes the tone grew heated between those who believed that leaving for *La Merica* was selling their soul to the devil, and those who, ticket in pocket—or almost—and daydreaming over glasses of grappa, laughed at their friends' timidity. *Over there ...*

How could anyone eavesdropping on all these tales avoid drifting off into the same dreams? They just needed to save enough money for the third-class crossing, so they could board one of the transatlantic liners like the ones on the posters plastered all around the port, the *Vulcania*, *Giulio Cesare*, *Conte di Savoia*, or *Aventino*, that took only three weeks to reach New York. Every passenger had to be in possession of the equivalent of a week's salary over there. Nella daydreamed along with all the others. She saved as much as she could of their meager income. The day she finally cobbled together the full sum she handed the money over for two tickets and then they left, each carrying a blanket and a canvas bag containing a few spare clothes, soap, and a hairbrush. What the letters home did not mention was that the crossing was hell, and that this hell continued after they arrived, and sometimes well beyond.

From what I understood, Nella had not, at first, wanted to go to America. The notion of another continent meant nothing to her, and her experience in the hold of the *Veloce* on the way over from Olbia to Naples had left her with ghastly memories. It was only when she saw Paolo being mocked, abused, and exploited by the men at the port, saw how he shut himself up more and more at night, and how he went down to the docks in the morning, his heart heavy and his feet dragging, that the dream of *La Merica* had seized her in turn, as it had so many others, and not let go. Leave, they had to leave. They had to find another life, a life that they could only have over there: she was convinced from the name of Little Italy that they would find identical landmarks as those in their native country.

All night I listened to Nella's hushed voice. I had no idea what to say. I'd have liked her to lie alongside me so I could watch her sleeping, I wanted nothing so much as to ease her suffering, but she remained wide awake, so tense it seemed she might break —despite her exhaustion and fear, and all the cruelty she had experienced. And I had behaved like a perfect swine, prepared to betray everything I believed in as a good officer of the Federal Immigration Service, a loyal and zealous servant of this great country of America, and damn the consequences. Nella had thrown me into utter disarray. I had wanted to be her savior, her good Samaritan, her guardian angel. And all I had succeeded in doing was to violate her, my sex erect and my breath ragged. Her brother had thrown himself out of a high window and she had cursed me. This was what I was going to have to live with now.

**ELLIS ISLAND, NOVEMBER 8,
9 O'CLOCK IN THE MORNING.**

As incomprehensible as it sounds, I have always refused to leave the island. I received several offers from the Federal Immigration Service to take up a more senior position, better paid and with more responsibility, and, most importantly, less isolated.

Three times I refused. To be seen as asocial, solitary, misanthropic, or lacking ambition mattered little to me. My standing was based on my vigilant and judicious management of this unique and ancient vessel moored a short distance from Manhattan. My reports arrived there like clockwork, and I even strived to augment them with proposals that went beyond my remit. On several occasions my suggestions were taken up, or became the starting point for subsequent decisions, which allowed me to remain in my post without any difficulty. It is true that there was no one really contesting me for the job. It's rare for someone to want to take on the role of the rat on a sinking ship. It may seem paradoxical, illogical, or even crazy to want to stay in a place where every day you are reminded of the worst time of your life. Perhaps it sounds like morbid complacency, or a peculiar taste for beyond the grave, but that was not it. It is fear that has kept me here. Fears, I should say, for they are multiple, ever-changing, and irrational. They are like a band of companions who never leave me alone, their teeth embedded in my flesh, digging in with every movement.

Between my dread and my hope of seeing Nella again, I'm no longer sure which one triumphs. When I try to work it out, I realize how ambivalent my feelings are. I looked for her for a long time. I miss her face; I'd like her to know that I meant what I said that night. I tried to find out where she was, how her life turned out. I haven't turned up a thing. Had things gone differently, would I have even had the courage—to beg forgiveness for taking advantage of her distress, and violating her like a brute; to throw myself at her feet and offer to make amends; to face her contempt and hatred? Nothing is straightforward. And yet I carried on looking for her. I consulted all the registers where she might be found: births, marriages, deaths, the Little Italy tabloids, records of mutual-aid societies, voluntary associations, parishes, lists of employees of different companies, directories of linen sellers, cooks, nursemaids, milliners, and seamstresses.

The few trips to Manhattan I allowed myself rarely had any other purpose. I never entered Little Italy, for fear of being recognized. Was that some paranoid fantasy? Physically I have changed. People often broaden and soften with age, but I have become tight, emaciated, stiff, and tense, as though my body has been suctioned in by some force. When it comes down to it, I'm not sure that if I were to cross paths with her someplace it would be more painful if she recognized me or had no idea who I was.

I must confess now that all these questions were nearly answered one summer's day a few years back when I thought I'd found her. It was summertime, that's all I'm sure of. For the rest, I get the years confused and I didn't have the heart to note down the date, which I still recall as an occasion of great pain and a complete fiasco.

I was sitting on a bench in a square near Little Italy, where I often stopped when I was in Manhattan. I had a little time before the ferry left. Looking up from my book, I noticed a young woman sitting on a nearby bench, just a few meters away, with her back to me. At her feet was a heavy shopping bag; she must have sat down for a moment to rest before continuing on her way home. I would have given ten years of my life to see her face. I sat and watched her for a long time. It was her hands that bothered me, I'd have known her hands from a thousand others. Swarthy, calloused, nervous, so unexpected in comparison to her slender figure. With the few available clues I tried to guess what her life might be like. I took note of her clothes: she wore a hat, and her shoes were plain, but decent quality and even modestly elegant. If it was indeed Nella, I was relieved to see that she was not one of those exhausted, dirt-poor women in a patched checkered skirt you see on streets all over the city, lugging huge baskets of dirty laundry all day long, or working in a sweatshop until they lose their sight, or washing floors and stairs, and then collapsing at night on a lousy mattress in a garret with no running water and walls sweating with damp.

It took me a split second to realize that this was the moment I had been waiting for, day and night, for so many years. There she was, so close at hand. Despite the trembling that seized me, despite the dizziness that blurred my vision, I was determined to go and speak to this young woman, without really knowing what I would say, though I'd imagined the scene a thousand times in the course of my sleepless nights. Just as I stood up, she lifted her hand to shield her eyes from the sun, which was when I knew with absolute certainty, from the grace of the movement, that it was Nella Casarini. And then I saw a glint of gold on her left hand. I sat down again, unable to move.

Two things were certain. It was Nella, and she was married. Was it possible that another man had been able to offer her what I had wanted to give her? Had he been able to make her forget those painful hours on Ellis Island? I hoped so, of course, yet the idea that she might have found happiness with someone else enraged me. And I had no idea if, after all these years, in the bright light of a summer morning, I had the right to force her to recall that terrible time. I closed my eyes for a moment to get a hold on myself and make some kind of decision. When I opened them again, the woman had gone. The only sign of her was the scuff in the sand left by her bag, by the bench where she had been sitting. I hadn't dreamed it. A few meters away, she'd already been absorbed into the crowd. I barely managed to stumble in her direction when I knocked into a passerby and was roundly insulted before eventually I gave up.

After the intensity of that glimpse of her, I returned to Ellis Island disoriented and distraught. Too many questions to which I'd never have an answer. Had Nella yielded to me merely out of desperation and necessity, hoping that her submission would perhaps help to obtain what she wanted most in the world for her brother and herself? Or was it possible that, in spite of everything, she had seen me as a man who wanted to love her? At that moment, I had been the only helping hand, the only sign of hope and humanity in an unfamiliar place with unknowable rules. And that outstretched hand had stolen everything from her. Is it possible that another man had known how to heal her wounds?

Nella is just a name on an Ellis Island register. Outside, just a few steps from Liz's grave, her brother's grave reminds me of her daily. The two tragedies of my life, side by side. And me between the two.

I was afraid, too, perhaps absurdly, that she might seek revenge. Solitude animates the imagination. The newspapers I receive here are filled with stories of Italian mafia crimes, with horrifying photographs of mutilated bodies lying on the sidewalk, frozen by death into grotesque, disturbing poses, a hat to one side, shoes to the other, rivulets of blood trickling beneath them. The work of hardened professionals, organized, armed, and merciless. I have often wondered if Nella might be in contact, one way or another, with other Italians close to the criminal organization. It was possible that the idea of revenge had been born in her, or that someone close to her had suggested it. Why not? Here I feel safe; in Manhattan, I am easy prey. Of course, I could have left New York and gone somewhere else to disappear. America is so vast. But I confess the idea never occurred to me.

On one occasion, the dread of seeing her name on a document was greater than the hope that I would find it there. It was the list of the victims of the terrible fire that took place in Little Italy in August 1939. One hot summer's day an entire block burned to the ground. It was one of those days when you can't imagine being able to deal with any more heat. Hell, but hotter. From Ellis Island you could see the thick black plumes of smoke rising over the city, and not a breath of air to chase them away. They seemed to have settled there for eternity. A tangle of buildings too close to one another, flammable materials, negligence, all the necessary elements for a small fire to turn into a tragedy. A wood-burning oven in some cheap joint, I think it was called Spaccanapoli, was likely left unattended, or overheated, and some cinders escaped that fed on anything they touched—wood, packaging, drapery. From the kitchen the fire spread to the dining room, and the neighboring buildings caught fire like paper. Twenty people died that day, in the toxic fumes inside carbonized walls, either trying to help or trapped by the fire that spread to all the neighboring houses, work-shops, and restaurants. The cries of desper-ate panic echoed for a long time in the rubble. I rushed to find out the names of the victims, visiting hospitals where the injured had been brought, consulting admission registers. At least my title had the advantage of opening doors by raising fears. Nella was not among the victims; I checked the identities of all the married women close to her age.

I returned to Ellis Island in a state of exhaustion I had rarely experienced; the acrid smell of smoke had penetrated my clothes, permeated my skin, and I felt like I would never get rid of it. I was sure of only one, important, fact: Nella had not been a victim of the disaster.

5 O'CLOCK IN THE AFTERNOON.

Over the years, the flood slowed to a trickle. The great era of immigration was over. Ellis Island was now more like a stagnant pond, where the occasional isolated case washed up, to be held in its buildings for varying periods and reasons.

Most of the workers had left, they had been offered other jobs by the federal services, or taken retirement. I knew none of the few remaining staff. I continued to roam the corridors and staircases, the deserted dormitories, the kitchens, and the infirmary. The Great Hall now welcomed only the wind and a few disoriented seagulls. In the rooms on the top floor remained some traces of the past: discarded belongings, clothes, empty trunks, torn blankets, broken tools, and dented musical instruments. There was an upright piano, which I think had always been there; I recall evenings listening to its music through the walls, like an indistinct echo. What does one take into exile? So little: only the things that really matter. The memory of certain melodies, the flavor of a particular food, a way of praying or greeting a neighbor. Sometimes an accordion or a guitar joined the piano, I could hear the music late into the night, as if the immigrants were able, in those moments, to resurrect fragments of their native lands for a few fleeting hours.

Apropos of this, there was one episode I've never forgotten. A comment by a German from Bremen or Hamburg, a wan, lumbering giant of a man who must have been an itinerant harvest worker back home, digging up beets and potatoes in exchange for a bowl of soup and a bed for the night. He came to my office for some reason, and at the end of our exchange he pointed to a sharp paper knife in a pencil pot and said a few words in his language that I didn't understand. I asked the interpreter who was with him, who looked both amused and embarrassed. *He says you must never put away a knife like that, his mother always says that an angel passing by might get hurt.* I looked with surprise at this man in his too-short jacket, kneading his cap in his hands. In a few words he had summoned his mother and the beliefs of his native region, and a whole world that he would never see again was suddenly intensely present in this room. What would become of him in a few years? I was in a good mood that day, I smiled and, to make him happy, I turned the paper knife so that it was pointing down in the pencil pot. I always store it like that now.

Although I kept myself to myself, I enjoyed the occasional festivities organized by the immigrants, as though yearning for a world where fraternity took the place of homeland. I was a very solitary person, and I realize now that over all those years I made very few friends or warm personal relationships. I've always been afraid of opening up to people, afraid I might not know when to stop, on an evening when everything might become too difficult, afraid of erasing the illusory protection that my position offered me, even though deep down I have never forgotten that I first came here as a lowly member of staff. A few faces fleetingly materialize as if emerging from a mist, before dissolving again—faces of those with whom I might, in another life, have liked to be friends, or at least to whom I might have been able to talk without fear of being judged, and without a position of superiority to maintain.

There was David Barry, one of the people responsible for immigrants' luggage, surprisingly quick-thinking in spite of his corpulence, who punctuated every sentence with his perpetual *Take it easy, man*, though ease was noticeably absent from this place. His work consisted of getting the new arrivals, already relieved of almost all their possessions, to deposit with him the few belongings they had arrived with, which they guarded like treasure. He had to convince them they would be able to pick them up again later, untouched, but there was always a good deal of shouting and resistance. There was Robert Hamilton, his face constantly twitching with tics and involuntary spasms, always nodding and chewing his lips, as if some snatch of inner conversation were trying to come to the surface; he always had just the right word or gesture to reassure people, though there was so little time for each new arrival; Margaret Price, the head nurse, who had huge round eyes in an angular face, like a child's drawing, and a heart much bigger than she cared to admit; and George Lawson, one of the physicians, possibly the person I felt closest to, a man of immense compassion, though it was often tempered by exhaustion. I was sorry to see him go, and even more sorry for the stiffness with which he came to say goodbye on the day of his departure. I was surprised; our relationship had always seemed to me cordial, even warm, and we were almost always in agreement when it came to handling different situations. I didn't understand his bearing that day, and I must admit I felt somewhat slighted. What did he even know about me?

Sometimes I had to take disciplinary measures and impose penalties, in the vast majority of cases for improper behavior motivated by greed. There were some unsavory cases of fraud, and a few truly despicable episodes—but that regards a term that I have difficulty using, because of what I had done to Nella. The fraud concerned the storing of luggage, the exchange of foreign for American money, and the inflation of the cost of train tickets sold to people leaving New York for distant cities such as Chicago, Pittsburgh, or Cleveland. Even the very poorest were ready to do anything they could to safeguard their few possessions. As for the racket I uncovered one day overcharging for the exchange of foreign money for dollars, it was appalling, as was the one in which a bed in a less crowded dormitory, or one equipped with better facilities, or an extra blanket, could be procured for a fee. I always insisted on the immediate dismissal of any member of my staff found guilty of extortion or bribery, and I hope no other wrongs were committed that passed me by; one thing to which I believe I can attest without fear of perjury is my utmost vigilance in that regard.

Who was I to all the men and women who worked here with me over the years? From time to time it seemed to me that in spite of the harshness of our daily lives, a harshness we each experienced in our own way, the atmosphere relaxed a little at holidays like Christmas and Thanksgiving, as if we all thirsted to forget the bleakness of Ellis Island for a few hours. Our daily routine would be sweetened by an improvised choir or a shared prayer. For the many Jewish immigrants it didn't mean much, they remained wide-eyed or indifferent spectators of these traditions, preferring to remain amongst themselves and trying, as best they could, to observe the weekly Sabbath, the Passover seder, Yom Kippur, and Hanukkah, and to consume only the food that complied with their religious precepts. Here, even the idea of God did not bring people together. I do not know whether He was silent, or if we were simply unable to hear Him.

There were also men with whom I experienced great difficulties. One does not choose one's company on board ship; in general it is authority that brings the members of a crew together, whether they are forced to accept it or seeking to defeat it; authority erases everything subjective in any personal relationship, be it hostile or sometimes unjust, which might disrupt the functioning of a set of complex workings that must never for any reason be interrupted. Ellis Island resembled nothing so much as a Ferris wheel tirelessly hauling its occupants in its cradle-like tubs, or a factory chain turning raw materials into finished products. Immigrants were plunged into the crucible that was Ellis, a gigantic baptismal font, to walk out as American citizens, free and equal, required to work hard, speak English, and use dollars in lieu of lire, zlotys, or rubles. It would be an illusion, however, to think that the men and women who contributed to the smooth running of this enterprise were no more than anonymous and interchangeable elements; to want to forget what was distinctive about each person would be like losing a fragment of one's soul.

I have to admit that I had a few colleagues with whom I would have preferred never to have crossed paths. Sherman was one; the mere thought of him fills me with bitterness and disgust. Augustus Frederick Sherman. How could I possibly forget him? I can still picture him, stout and saturnine, with his prophet's beard, round glasses, self-righteous expression, and prying eyes, constantly on the lookout. He was Chief Registry Clerk, in charge of the twenty men who dealt with the station's correspondence; we devoured paper like ogres at Ellis Island. We worked closely together, and he had to report to me every day. I sensed a muted, simmering rivalry, even jealousy, towards me. He had a complex, I think, about his civilian status, subordinate to my commissioner's livery. His personal ambition and pride could barely tolerate his position; I suspect he found it humiliating to be confined to doing thankless paperwork, unable to influence any concrete decisions to be made.

He ran his section along strict, even harsh lines, insisting that his men worked in complete silence, and he instituted a complicated ceremony, worthy of a Sultan, when it came to him being disturbed. Photography began as a hobby that became an obsession, and in later years it brought him a certain renown. He wore an aura of great importance when he went off to take pictures at the end of his working day. I didn't have the authority to forbid him from taking his endless photographs of the immigrants being held at Ellis Island. My predecessor had tolerated, perhaps even encouraged it. When I became commissioner, I found myself with no say in the matter, for it was by then an established habit that was hard for me to challenge. And after all, what objection could I have made? His work wasn't affected. His photographs brought him the recognition he had long dreamed of—how validated he felt when they appeared in *National Geographic*. You had to see his triumphant expression. I certainly wasn't jealous of him. I just didn't like the fellow, that's all.

Sherman the photographer was frequently accompanied by his crony Luigi Chianese the interpreter, with his useful polyglot skills. I hated seeing them together, they were like some sinister, silent force, a two-headed being both well-matched and ill-assorted, as they prowled the corridors during their after-dark expeditions. My authority had little hold over them, and I couldn't quite put my finger on what it was they were brewing. If I consider the facts objectively, the two hundred or so photographs Sherman left are part of the memory of Ellis Island, testifying to the reality of the new arrivals and their fates. Families with innumerable children, standing stiffly in front of the lens in their best clothes, in a stunning demonstration of the breadth of our nation's welcome. *God bless America!* Certainly, if we didn't have them, what would we know of those millions of people who arrived here with fifty dollars in their pocket, speaking not a word of English, who slowly became assimilated into America's soil, contributing to its glory and wealth? There was nothing in his project

I could object to. But his photographs made me uncomfortable. I knew what was behind them, and I knew too well the way the two men worked, how intrusive and insistent they were. You had to see Sherman, as soon as he had tidied up his folders of mail and stacks of documents, how he would spend long hours peering into individual faces and considering groups of people. It seemed to me to be a form of harassment, a shameful pursuit.

I know how determined he was once he had identified an individual, a couple, or a family. An *ethnic type*, as he used to put it. His potential models could not of course refuse to be photographed, as they had no idea whether or not it was required. He addressed those who were being held here for an indefinite period, either for medical reasons or for further interrogation. These were people in situations of complete insecurity, who faced the very real risk of being refused access through the golden door. Their faces were warped with fatigue, disfigured by anxiety and anticipation; entire families penned in by his lens, frightened children, exhausted mothers with babies in their arms, fathers watching over them all with benevolence and resolve. Many had never seen a camera before in their life.

I was told that often Sherman would rifle through their suitcases and trunks, looking for native costumes, elaborate headdresses, unusual jewelry, traditional tunics or boots, ornate belts, and other emblems of traditions and customs that were so different to ours. Perhaps I am badly placed to judge such practices and play the sensitive soul, but I certainly would not have been able to harass those wretched people, day after day, to dress up in their native attire. Sherman turned an unused room into a studio, in which he kept the large tripod camera that was necessary for the long exposures. There was a black or a white curtain for a backdrop, depending on the complexion and clothing of his subjects. In an adjoining room, which was no more than a small closet, he set up a darkroom for developing his photographs. All I know of his background is that he was born in

Pennsylvania, and that he and his family were members of the Episcopal Church. How he'd gotten here, I have no idea. But what I do know, and this is the main reason for my reservations about him, is that his anthropological portraits were published by journals promoting racialist propaganda. I don't know whether or not this was with his consent, but I am sure it would not have been possible unless he himself had provided the images. These journals sought to use photography to demonstrate the disparities between races and the inferiority of some of them, using the pictures as a call for America to wake up, and for immigration from abroad to be limited. They campaigned for strict selection criteria for immigrants, and condemned entire ethnic groups for supposedly corrupting our country. This wrongheaded exploitation of racial types using an anthropometric approach horrified me.

I told him this during a meeting at which I rebuked him for allowing the publication of the portraits without having sought permission from the authorities at Ellis.

These were, after all, professional documents, which could be considered confidential. He didn't answer, and a heavy silence settled between us. I told him that it must not happen again, and stood up to signify that our meeting had come to an end. I didn't look at him. A year later he retired, and a few months after that I learned of his death.

The difficulty of our relationship peaked during the drama concerning Nella. We came close to a fight, and I must say I would not have been sorry had I broken his jaw or smashed his skull, but he withdrew before I had the pleasure. During the wake for young Paolo, all the Italians were gathered in a room outside the main building that was reserved for this somber purpose, and lit only by candles placed around the body, which the women had tried to make presentable; everyone was dressed in black, standing around the coffin, reciting prayers and singing mournful hymns. Then Sherman turned up with his tripod and his photographic plates. I was standing at the back by the door, not knowing what else to do. When I saw him, I was livid. I could not imagine how anyone could do such a thing. I stood blocking the entrance, my muscles coiled, ready to lunge at him. *Looking for something, are you, Mr. Sherman?* He stopped, slightly out of breath with the weight of his equipment, and wiped his forehead with a large handkerchief. He revolted me. I knew I would have done something violent if I had surprised him a few minutes later already busy with his scavenging. I took a step forward. *Beat it, right now! Don't you dare think about trying to come inside. I'll kill you if you try.* From the frightened surprise I read on his face, I knew he wouldn't take the risk. The Italians had noticed nothing through their tears and prayers, and Nella had no idea I was even there.

ELLIS ISLAND, NOVEMBER 9,
7 O'CLOCK IN THE MORNING.

This morning, I don't know why, Francesco Lazzarini's face came to mind. The enigmatic, skeptical expression etched on his gaunt face, his lean body and measured movements. I recalled the way he used to light his cigarette in an unhurried ritual, as though he were bestowing on himself a reward that he intended to enjoy to the full; between puffs, he would stare thoughtfully at the glowing tip, as if it held some kind of secret. Not the kind of man you'd want to pick a fight with. I sensed, in his considered gestures, a capacity for rapid reaction, silent and swift.

Lazzarini was one of the passengers on the *Cincinnati* that had brought over Nella and her brother. Something about his status was unclear, which had led to him being detained here while we waited for clarifications. If the papers he had with him were genuine, he was a good deal younger than he appeared. According to his papers he was only thirty, but he looked at least fifteen years older. He was a carpenter by trade, and in answer to our questioning he told us it was hunger, poverty, and laboring in the open air that had etched the deep lines in his face and stretched his skin taut over his bones.

Perhaps this was true. In all other respects we had no issue with him. Accustomed to deprivation and seeking shelter wherever he could, he'd have been happy with his accommodation at Ellis Island were it not for the constant, gnawing uncertainty about his future.

He arrived here with just his tools in a waxed canvas bag. Carpenters like him were in great demand at the time, in this metropolis that seemed more like a vast building site than a settled, finished city, which I don't think it will ever be. Lazzarini was waiting for the authorities in his hometown, Rossano, in Calabria, I seem to recall, to confirm that he was indeed born on the date marked on his identity papers. I had wondered about the possibility that he had stolen someone else's identity. The way he had of fingering the knife he often held in his hand, his habit of chiseling away at a piece of wood from morning to night, his intense, taciturn demeanor, a kind of inner tension that looked like it could be released in a flash, like a coiled spring, made his presence vaguely unnerving. I wondered if there had been a fight, a settling of scores. A knife in the belly that in an instant turns a man into a murderer. All that remains is to steal the victim's papers and flee. Perhaps he believed that the law would forget about him once he'd gotten to the other side of the world. I was suspicious, unnecessarily so perhaps, but this kind of investigation was part of my job. Meanwhile Lazzarini suffered in silence.

One night a storm tore off an entire section of the roof and smashed a great number of windowpanes, and we didn't have enough men to complete the most urgent repairs. Lazzarini stopped me in the corridor and managed to make me understand, with hand gestures and a few words in broken English, that he would like to help. To his surprise, I responded in Italian, accepting his proposal. We were short of people. After that we occasionally exchanged a few words. To be honest, it was always I who found a pretext to speak to him or summon him to my office for one reason or another—for further information, to discuss some new development in his case, or some other nonsense I'd invented. All this had only one purpose. Lazzarini had crossed paths with Nella and I was desperate to find out everything he knew about her, everything he had seen, heard, or guessed during the terrible crossing. That was all that interested me. Without the link to Nella perhaps I would not have been so exacting regarding the inconsistencies in his paperwork. One day, sitting behind my desk in my uniform, I put on my most serious and stern expression, and brought the conversation round to Nella and her unfortunate brother. *I imagine you are aware of the tragedy that took place here a few weeks ago. What do you know of the young woman and her brother?* I was behaving like a prosecutor, a grand inquisitor, Cato and Torquemada entwined. If he had known how I was trembling ... His words shook me to the core.

Yes, they had indeed both been passengers in the *Cincinnati*'s squalid steerage on the voyage from Naples, in April 1923. Nella and her brother made a distinctive pair: she with her tall, slender figure, olive skin, and green eyes; and Paulo, who never took so much as a step away from her side, a docile Hercules with the features of a child. But it was for another entirely different reason during those dreadful days at sea that he took notice of Nella and would remember her until the day he died. His account sent a shiver through me.

Passengers in steerage had to go down into the ship's hold, where the conditions were horrific, by a narrow staircase with slippery steps as steep as a ladder. No ventilation, men and women separated by no more than a dirty drape, two sinks, a narrow cot for each person, no drinking water, rank food doled out from enormous kettles into metal bowls that the passengers had to procure at their own expense, and the overwhelming stench of cooking, tobacco, wine, sweat, disinfectant, hundreds of bodies crammed into a confined space, engine oil, and the permanent vibration of the engines. Nothing to do all day other than to pray upon waking that the time would pass as swiftly as possible, to count the hours and hope—that the next sunrise would herald a calm sea so that they would not suffer too much from seasickness, that no one would steal their belongings, that they wouldn't fall and injure themselves, that they would eventually arrive. Hope. Every morning trying to forget the day before, desperate for it to be swallowed up into the pit of days, into a space beyond memory, into the black hole of consciousness where only forgetting makes it possible to carry on.

Lazzarini would become very agitated when he spoke of those terrible days. Then he would fall silent, drawn back to that place from which he summoned up images lodged deep in his memory, bringing them to light with great caution. About a week before they reached New York, an extraordinary thing happened. He muttered something in a dialect that I didn't understand, Calabrian or Neapolitan, then resumed his story.

One evening, after dinner, we heard a child

scream, a cry of terrible pain, and then a woman shrieking and a great commotion throughout the hold. Everyone yelling and running in all directions trying to find a doctor, "Un medico! Un medico!" *The word was relayed like a great wave from one end to the other of the confined space below deck. A doctor! Yes, there was a doctor on board, just one for two thousand four hundred people; it was pathetically inadequate. Moreover, the ship's doctor generally only attended to passengers in first class: ladies with the vapors, seasickness, digestive problems. It was hard to imagine the medical officer walking through the large, brightly lit lounges, ballrooms, and dining rooms, and entering the mahogany-paneled cabins, carrying with him the stench of his recent visit to third class, his shoes stained with vile, mysterious matter.*

But a doctor was needed, although I am not sure he would have been able to do much. A child of five or six called Lorenza, the daughter of a Neapolitan couple, Vittore and Gabriella Battini, a stonemason and a seamstress, had been horribly burned. She'd been playing with the other children; all they were trying to do was escape the boredom, inactivity, and sea-sickness; she'd slipped under the guardrail in front of a white-hot stove and tried to hide in the tiny space between the stove and the wall. She'd flattened herself against the metal and all the skin on her back had burned off. The mother could do nothing but wail, horrified by the sight of her child's raw flesh, and the child had lost consciousness from the pain.

When Nella realized what had happened, she jumped up and made her way through the agitated crowd. Up until then she had been simply a reserved young woman taking care of her simple-minded brother, hardly noticed by anyone else. Now she had an air of authority and confidence that struck everyone who saw her. "Let me through." Instinctively, the crowd parted to allow her to pass. She glanced neither right nor left, making her way towards the child as quickly as she could.

When she reached Lorenza, who was lying on her front, she gestured to the circle of curious, shocked people leaning over the child to make space. Everyone took a few steps back and the circle reformed identically a few meters away. Then she knelt down beside Lorenza, *who had regained consciousness, but had not even enough strength to moan. She wept silent tears, tears the size of pearls. Nella held her hands open above the child's body and moved them slowly through the air, tracing the line of her back, whispering indistinct words in a low voice. An absolute silence descended; only the dull thrum of the engines could be heard. She stayed kneeling for a long time, her eyes intensely focused, and suddenly she began to grimace as though in pain, and then she collapsed, and her face relaxed. She looked exhausted. I was standing facing her a few meters away. In all my life, I have never witnessed anything so astonishing. Lorenza had fallen quiet. She stopped moaning, her face was calm, and she fell asleep.*

Nella asked Lorenza's mother for a clean cloth, which she placed gently over the child's wounded flesh, then she beckoned the father to pick her up and carry her to her cot. Nella left as she had come, but this time the crowd parted of its own accord. She was reeling with fatigue and shivering despite the stifling heat in steerage. Someone supported her and walked her back to her cot. I was not so bold. She silently expressed her thanks with a blink of her eyelids, and fell almost immediately into a deep sleep. Her brother sat at the foot of her cot, one hand resting on hers, humming to himself a kind of nursery rhyme and gazing into empty space.

The following day something quite unbelievable took place. When the child awoke, her wounds were almost entirely healed; it was barely possible to see any trace of them. People fell to their knees, and though it went against all my convictions, I did too. From this moment on, Nella was regarded as a heroine, a saint, to be protected by us all. Donations poured in, we had almost nothing, but everyone considered it an honor to give her what little they had. Clothes, money—if she had accepted it all, she would have needed a caravan of mules to bring it all off the boat.

Yes indeed, sir, Nella Casarini was someone quite out of the ordinary. She knew the gestures and words that heal, and she could see deep inside things to understand their workings. Where we come from, everyone knows such powers have two sides, and that their other side is black as night. We feared Nella Casarini as *much as we venerated her, because we were ignorant and afraid, though, like me, everyone would tell you what a beautiful soul she had.*

Francesco Lazzarini stopped talking. I thought he had come to the end of his story, but I saw that some powerful emotion was preventing him from continuing. I was stunned, I felt faint, and I tried to turn the conversation back to more concrete matters. *Come, Signor Lazzarini, you seem to me to be a very rational man, surely this is no more than a romantic fiction.* He stared at me for a long time without saying a word.

ELLIS ISLAND, NOVEMBER 10,
4 O'CLOCK IN THE MORNING.

The Rossano Town Hall finally came back to us with information about Lazzarini. By what chance did I find myself there one morning, just when the clerks were sorting through the morning mail that had been brought over on the ferry boat, ready to distribute it among the different services? The letter from Rossano was not addressed to me personally, and it ought to have gone first to an interpreter to be speedily translated, then put in the pigeonhole of the clerk in charge of Italian immigrants. It was the large envelope that caught my attention, with its old-fashioned calligraphy, the capitals curved, wide and tall, each letter perfectly formed, all sealed with red wax and a thin cord. Intrigued, amused even, I took a closer look at this curious object. It was the commune of Rossano that was honoring us with this delivery. I picked up the envelope while the junior clerks, perhaps intimidated by the unusual fact of my presence, focused industriously on their task of sorting the mail. I went back to my office, the letter from Rossano in my hand. I wanted to know what information it contained about Lazzarini. He intrigued me and I was convinced he was no ordinary immigrant waiting to be regularized. I admit that the answer, though it was certainly illuminating, came as a complete surprise, and I found myself, for the first time in my entire professional life, faced with a moral dilemma.

Francesco Lazzarini had not lied about his date of birth; in spite of his appearance, he was indeed the age he claimed to be. He was not a professional assassin or even a one-time murderer, a mundane individual who had pulled out his knife even before he had realized he needed to. He was altogether worse. The Rossano Town Hall, in a formulation as overblown as the inscription on the envelope, considered it their duty to bring to our attention some information that may prove helpful regarding any decision we might take about Mr. Lazzarini. Attached to the letter, as proof, were some yellowing newspaper clippings stuck on large sheets of paper with the name and date of the publication at the top and center.

Lazzarini was an anarchist and had by all accounts been closely involved in the organization of a labor protest in Naples six months earlier. The demonstration, which was intended to be peaceful, had gone wrong. The provocations of the protestors? The response of the police? Soldiers, sent in as support, opened fire and several protesters were seriously injured, as well as one of the *carabinieri*, who had been separated from his troop by the demonstrators and drawn down a dark alley, where he died under a rain of blows. There were multiple arrests and convictions, and Lazzarini's name circulated. Either someone had informed on him, or he was already known to the police and under surveillance because of his activities.

The man was never found, but during a search of his room, a miserable hovel he shared with one of his anarchist comrades, the police seized a large quantity of leaflets and copies of a periodical dedicated to their cause. Had he merely taken part in the demonstration or was he one of the organizers? Was he anything to do with the lynching of the unfortunate *carabiniere*? Nothing was proven, but all the evidence suggested that Lazzarini was indeed a militant anarchist, and thus a wanted man, and the weight of the evidence against him was such that he risked spending the rest of his life in prison. I put the clippings down, shocked. I thought of the man who had told me the secret of Nella, the man who had worked for two days and two nights in a row, taking no rest, helping the workers to repair the roof, the windows, and the rooms damaged in the storm, with great skill, in silence, completely focused on his task. Sometimes he would use hand gestures to show our workmen what to do to, and the immigrants who slept in the damaged part of the building, who had had to be hastily evacuated and bedded down in even worse conditions, were soon able to recover some semblance of comfort in their dormitories. Unassuming and reserved, he accepted the beer and cigarettes that the workmen offered him, and returned to his solitude as soon as the work was completed, without in any way seeking to profit from this unexpected rapprochement, to fraternize or gain any kind of advantage from the situation.

Even before the letter arrived, I had made the decision to release Lazzarini and let him try his luck here in America. It seemed to me that I owed him that, but the letter from Rossano threw a new and disturbing light on him and his situation. The man had been deeply affected by Nella's gifts, however much it went against his beliefs—that was how I understood what he had told me. Had he really murdered a man during a riot, or encouraged someone else to? What danger did he represent to his own country or to ours? In Europe the threat from anarchists was real, their violent assaults were multiplying, they were considered evil incarnate—and Lazzarini was one of them.

I sat quite still at my desk for a long time. I was utterly nonplussed. I was here to defend my country, to protect it from just this kind of criminal element, whose activities risked spreading across America if they were allowed in. If I did not prevent them from entering the country and becoming American citizens, what was the purpose of the station, with all its staff, its strict organization, its complex and Byzantine procedures? No point, no point at all. Of course, we could provide no guarantee regarding the morality, intentions, and future conduct of any newcomers, at most we could be relatively sure that we were not allowing any proven dangerous elements to enter our territory. I struggled for a long time with these questions, thinking of the barbarity of the incipient Italian-American mafia that was made up of individuals who had arrived here entirely legally. I always came back to the same conclusion. I had decided to release Lazzarini. The debt that I owed him could not be repaid in any other way.

After a few days, I managed to get over this agonizing state of inner tension that had engulfed me, and asked for Lazzarini to be sent to my office, alone, without an interpreter. He stood in the doorway, his features impassive. I beckoned him inside, and told the employee who had accompanied him to return to work. I had no intention of playing cat and mouse with him. The situation was already sufficiently trying for me. I motioned for him to sit down and put before him the documents from Rossano, the letter and the cuttings from the *Gazzetta di Napoli* and the *Corriere del Sud*. I sensed him falter slightly, his jaw clenching almost imperceptibly, but his face gave nothing away. He read through the documents then looked at me without a word, as if to say, *Well, now you know everything, what are you going to do?*

Was he innocent? Guilty? A simple carpenter with dubious sympathies, or a militant blinded by his cause, a fanatical assassin? I didn't know what to think, but one thing was certain: before I dealt with him, one way or another, I wanted to know who I had sitting before me. *Mr. Lazzarini, there is one aspect of your story I don't understand. How, given that the police were after you, did you manage to board the boat? You needed to produce documents to be allowed on board, and you weren't a stowaway. Can you explain this?* Lazzarini's case was a genuine conundrum. It was clear that he alone could explain what had happened. He might lie to me, of course, but I knew enough now, it seemed to me, to be able to distinguish truth from falsehood. I felt Lazzarini's smoldering presence, impenetrable and steely, like white-hot stone, his deep, dark eyes seeming to weigh up his interlocutor, ready to grasp his innermost thoughts. His presence was too intense, too untamable for this bureau of the American administration, with its filing cabinets and pens all neatly lined up. There was something irreducible about him, a sense of unarticulated threat, all the more strange given that at that moment the man was at my mercy. The net was closing in on him, but nothing seemed to undermine his poise. In spite of his shabby clothes, his torn shirt, and rope sandals, there was something noble about Lazzarini.

Allow me to explain what happened, Signor Mitchell. It's time to tell the truth at last. It was all very straightforward. I came on board with papers that did not belong to me. An excellent forgery, by comrades who were the very best in their field. As far as my appearance went, I simply let my beard grow and cut my hair short, nothing more, but enough to transform a man. My comrades gave me a pair of shoes and a coat; I looked almost like a gentleman. And you must know, signore, even if it sheds no glory on the reputation of my compatriots, the carabinieri responsible for checking passengers' papers as they boarded grew rather less conscientious after a good lunch and a few shots of grappa. Once again, this was thanks to my comrades. You know how it's done: they frequented the same taverna, found themselves chatting to some strangers at a neighboring table, saw them again the next day and the one after that, and ended up drinking together and gathering information, all suspicions lulled.

I interrupted him: *Where were you during those days?*

Operating as a clandestine is a skilled occupation, Signor Mitchell. The important thing is to have several hiding places and never spend more than one day or one night in each. I waited. When the time was right, I presented myself to the officials at the foot of the steps that led up to the gangplank. I went at the busiest time, stood among the large families, parents, children, other relatives, with their suitcases, trunks, and packages, amid all the yelling and wailing. There was an enormous crowd, and the carabinieri had little time for each passenger. I showed my papers with my name, Carlo Palacci, Neapolitan builder, said I was going to join my fiancée who had left with her parents a few months earlier. I even showed them letters from America!

I listened to Lazzarini, not quite sure what to think. The man had put his cards on the table with surprising candor. Yet I had the impression that he was guiding me deep into the heart of a forest, showing me the path he had chosen, and that at some point he would disappear, leaving me behind. I pulled myself together. *You came here under your own name, you used your real identity, while you apparently traveled under the name of another passenger, a certain Carlo Palacci, also Italian, traveling alone like yourself, and of course we have found no trace of him disembarking. What made you take this risk? Surely you knew information would be sent on ahead of you?*

Lazzarini said nothing for a long moment. *Perhaps, but not necessarily. The proof is that you have only just received it.* He fell silent and closed his eyes, as if searching for the right words or trying to extract a deep, buried memory.

The truth is a little different, Signor Mitchell. Lazzarini is my name, and that of my father, my grandfather, and of generations of men who have lived upstanding lives, poor but honest, proud of their name and their work. That is my blood and my inheritance. Whatever fate awaited me here, I decided to face it without hiding behind a name that was not mine. Carlo Palacci's papers ended up in the ocean, Lazzarini took back his name, and the coat and shoes went to a young man who needed them more than I. As far as the rest is concerned, I did take part in the protest, but I was at the head of the procession and, yes, I sang loudly, but the tragedy happened at the back. I only learned about it half an hour later. When the police charged us, I still knew nothing of it. That is all I have to tell you, Signor Mitchell.

He closed his eyes again, and when he opened them, they were shining so brightly I couldn't look into them.

Without a word, I drew out of a drawer the document that would authorize him to enter American territory as an American citizen. He watched as I tore up the cuttings and the letter, keeping only the birth certificate that was attached to it. *There's a ferry to Manhattan in less than an hour. Take your things and go.* He looked at me and then inclined his head slightly, and closed his eyes for a moment. I heard him say, *Grazie, tankiou.* I had nothing to add. I said simply, *Please go.* He turned back to look at me as he walked out the door, *Addio, Signor Mitchell.*

Alone again, I sat and tore the documents into tiny shreds, letting them fall through my fingers like confetti. In a few short minutes, I had done nothing less than betray my country.

10 O'CLOCK IN THE MORNING.
With Lazzarini, just as with Nella, I had crossed a line to a place from which there was no possibility of return. I had to find a way to compensate for my guilt at having allowed an individual representing a potential danger to our society to enter the country, and for reasons that were scarcely honorable. I had somehow to find a way to make up for my actions. I had chosen to believe that Lazzarini, deeply shaken by the scene he had witnessed on the boat, and perhaps motivated by the fact that I had

given him a chance, would decide to follow a different path. I have never been able to find out.

And so I decided to return to being the inflexible sentinel I had once been. The time was ripe for it. Since the Russian Revolution of 1917 and the spectacular rise of communism and antisemitism in Europe, many intellectuals and artists had been forced into exile, fleeing persecution in their homelands. America was desperate to protect itself from communism, and hunted down people who held such beliefs, even those who were no longer welcome in their own countries for being too free in their ways of thinking. It was impossible to entertain the thought of them being allowed entry here.

Our embassies regularly drew up lists of suspects likely to knock at the golden door. Even though they carried out preliminary interrogations and it was they who decided whether or not to authorize candidates for exile to set sail for America, the system had loopholes. So I became a zealous hunter of Reds. I believed that this way I might redeem myself, for the good of my country and the honor of my uniform. What foolishness, what vanity! It was the episode of the Hungarian writer György Kovács and his wife Esther that led me to understand, many years later, with a horror that still resonates in me today, that idealism is always on the side of the human spirit, guilt on the side of power, and history is always the only judge.

Despite being a dissident, György Kovács was on a list of communist intellectuals sent by our ambassador in Budapest. As soon as he and his wife arrived at Ellis Island, they were subjected to a tense series of interrogations, and the decision was made to deny them entry. I can picture them now, standing in a huddled embrace, as if keeping each other from being swept away by the wind and the waves. Neither was particularly tall. They were both gaunt and serious-looking, she even more gaunt than he in her trim gray skirt and jacket, a simple silver brooch, and a rustic pair of boots; he in an overcoat with an upturned collar, a hat, and silver-rimmed spectacles.

They walked together to the dock, let their eyes wander over the line of Manhattan skyscrapers, then turned around and walked back, still holding each other, their twin silhouettes grave and unspeaking. Esther spent a few days in the infirmary for some minor indisposition. Kovács walked around alone those days, as if quite lost. He sat outside on a bench and scribbled feverishly in the notebook he kept in his pocket. They had applied for visas to Brazil and were waiting for the response. They didn't know how long they were going to spend in this transit camp, so close to their dream, a dream that stood right before their eyes, staring them down all day long.

They eventually left for Latin America. An odd couple. They might have inspired pity, yet they did not. His face was filled with intelligence, energy, and focus. She was distant, dignified, patient, and calm, despite her apprehension and their miserable circumstances. I was struck by a comment he made during our final interview, when I told him that they would be able to go to Brazil. I had forgotten to put the accents on his name on various documents. He reproached me gently but firmly, and I will never forget his words: *We have nothing left, sir, except the certainty that we will remain exiles until the end of our days, far from the world where we were born and grew up, far from our native language. Must you deprive us even of the accents in our names?* Then he smiled, with a discomfiting sadness. I didn't know what to answer, and simply rectified the error, like a schoolboy who had been caught out.

It was not until fifteen years later, well after the end of the war, that the echo of this forgotten conversation came back to me. I was leafing through the *New York Times* one day, when I came across a lengthy, laudatory review of one of Kovács's books that had just been translated into English, as had most of his work, I discovered, as well as into many other languages. It was a collection of reflections on the theme of exile. The author, according to the article, had been living in Latin America for many years, and this was the first time he had written about exile. *Fragments of Exile* was, said the reviewer, a deeply affecting book, at once the most personal and yet the most universal book by this immensely important writer to whom our country had failed to offer asylum.

Kovács's intense, melancholy expression, his glasses, hat, and overcoat, instantly came back to me. He had been here in this very room, dignified and weary, and he had still managed to find the courage to smile about the missing accents in his name. I had to read this book. I went to Manhattan, to the downtown bookstore on Broadway where three or four times a year I would go to pick up a pile of books to take back with me to Ellis Island. The bookseller knew nothing of what I did for a living, I always went in civilian clothes, and never told him anything about myself. He must have thought me an odd character, in my old-fashioned suit with a fitted, buttoned-up jacket, who lived far away and only rarely came to the city. I was quite happy that way.

György Kovács's book was displayed in the window along with his other books, and there was a stack of copies on a table near the counter. I didn't even have to ask for it; I simply took a copy and placed it with feigned indifference on top of the other books I'd chosen. The bookseller—an affable man, as talkative as he was slow, as if his body and his speech didn't move at the same pace, each endowed with an independence that allowed them to lead a distinct existence—decided to engage me in conversation. More than once he had put a book in my hands with an air of authority, *Take this, you won't be disappointed.* How could he know what I was expecting from a book, how could he gauge what would disappoint me, or not? It was a mystery without consequence. He glanced approvingly at the Kovács and looked me up and down before breaking into a smile. I got the impression I'd passed a test, without knowing either the question or the criteria for evaluating the answer. *Kovács*, he repeated thoughtfully. *Yes, you really have to read that.* I wanted to get away as quickly as possible, so I picked up my bundle of books with the air of a man who has suddenly remembered he has an appointment in fifteen minutes at the other end of town. Read Kovács. I had no idea what awaited me.

Kovács wrote about his life in exile, uprooting, displacement, discouragement, fear of the unknown, fear of forgetting his language, nostalgia for the music of his native land, the cafés of Budapest and the view of the Danube from the Fisherman's Bastion, the strength of the love that bound him to Esther, without whom, he avowed, he would never have had the courage to write the most difficult book of his career. He wrote about the United States and the golden door, dreamed of, glimpsed, and slammed shut in his face. Kovács also wrote about Ellis Island in a fragment entitled *The Island of Twenty-Nine Questions*.

Our dream of Atlantis, or Mount Ararat, where our ark would finally wash ashore, our hope of an Ithaca where our weary bodies and souls might finally find a place to rest, was reduced to a goblet of bitterness, a nightmare drenched in mist and damp, in freezing, inhospitable barracks. The America we had so longed for was reduced to a camp of harried, timorous officials charged with keeping at bay any attempt to approach a different way of thinking, any seed of possible intellectual non-conformity. America knew how to open her arms wide, and she showed us that she knew how to snap them shut just as abruptly. That was the only America we were permitted to encounter before we continued our journey of wandering and hope across the seas of the world.

That was where I chanced upon a strange irony of fate, or a confusing manifestation of the theory of relativity: I had been persecuted because I was insufficiently communist, too critical of a blind and brutal system, not communist enough to be allowed to remain in my own country, and at the same time I was far too communist to be allowed into America, where the very word terrifies even those men on the street who are utterly ignorant of and indifferent to any kind of public discourse. To get so close to a dream and to see it vanish before one's eyes, even as it is right there before you, so real and so close, is a strange experience. For Esther and me, the golden door will forever remain a portcullis made of steel.

And while the Sphinx of Thebes asked but a single question before devouring any unfortunate unable to provide the answer, American officials do even better, since it is only after twenty-nine questions that they swallow the reprobate into the limbo of their statistics and send them back to sea. One can only imagine the fragility, the mad energy, the distress, and the determination of all those who, one day, in order to escape misery or persecution, agreed to give everything up, in order, perhaps, to gain it all back at the price of one of the most terrible mutilations there is: the loss of homeland, family, the repudiation of their native language, and sometimes of even their own name, the price of forgetting all their traditions and songs. For only by consenting to this mutilation will the golden door swing open.

Oscillating between memory and nostalgia, as between Scylla and Charybdis, these people had to move forward and forget in order to survive. It was at Ellis Island, that melancholy alambic, that the first signs of this transmutation took place, yes, at Ellis Island, the *grotto of oblivion and renunciation, inside those buildings wide open to the winds of suffering and despair. Ellis Island, the stepping-stone to a longed-for country and the dream of a new life. And in this non-place, the guardians of the temple are busy. Endless doctors in white coats eradicating lice, like beasts of burden responsible for the smooth circulation of this anthill. At Ellis Island time no longer exists, waiting becomes the only measure. You who enter here, know that all watches and clocks have stopped, you cannot know whether you will be here for hours or for several long weeks, you will measure the duration of your visit hour by hour, day by day.*

Forget, forget everything you know, and give thanks to munificent America, which swallows you up like Jonah, deep inside its belly, before spitting you out into this unknown land that will become yours; you will be its salt and its soil, for in exchange for America's magnanimity, you must offer up your sweat, your blood, and your lack of any regret. Who can distinguish between the banks of the Hudson that embrace you, and those of Lethe? But will you still remember, brother—when your own children can barely understand the language that was once yours—the language of your father, your mother, and all your ancestors, the songs of the women of your village and the color of the sky on harvest days? I knocked at the golden door and it did not swing open for me. Was I really such a threat to the great country of America? Were Esther and I, reeling with exhaustion and sorrow, really such a danger? I cannot believe we were. Today I have no regrets, no rancor, for here, in the place where we came to land, we found, at last, fraternity and compassion.

I could not read on. I closed the book and wept.

The final evening. Tomorrow I am leaving. Last night, I had the same recurring dream I have had for many years. I dread it, for every time I wake up from it I am undone, as if I had spent the entire night battling something terrifying; but I look forward to it, too, for Nella's face appears to me with such clarity and precision that I am convinced I can take her in my arms and beg her forgiveness; the vision fades at dawn, when I greet the day's dull colors and sharp contours with utter despondency.

In my dream, Nella is standing on the pier down by Battery Park; she has been pacing the waterfront since dawn. She watches the horizon, waiting for me. I arrive by boat, as I get closer I can see her, brisk and slender as a brushstroke, her bright-colored dress, her beribboned hat. The boat speeds up, then begins to slow, taking a wide curve as it approaches the dock, but it never arrives. Nella is waiting for me and I can do nothing to warn her, I am condemned to leave her there, waiting for all eternity. And then I awaken, my heart thumping.

It is almost nightfall. Enough of memories; from tomorrow I will have all my days and nights to devote to them. Tomorrow morning the men appointed to close down the station are coming to take me back to Manhattan. It will be night still when they arrive, and mooring in the dark is unsafe; I need to replace the bulb in the lantern at the end of the dock. I should have dealt with it earlier. Fortunately there is no wind tonight. I have just enough time to take a ladder down from the workshop and fix it before it will be too dark to see.

The men from the Federal Immigration Service discovered the body upon their arrival the following morning. It was floating alongside the pontoon, and they spotted it even before they came close to land. A dark, heavy, down jacket, pulled on over the uniform, had kept the body floating at the surface, like a buoy. As soon as they'd gotten off the ferry the men pulled the body out of the water and straightaway recognized it as the commissioner. Accidental drowning, it was pretty obvious. The ladder was still leaning against the streetlamp. A box of tools lay open on the ground.

Andrew Logan, the coroner, was dispatched immediately to the scene. He was around thirty, all arms and legs; the hat perched lopsidedly on his head and his hastily belted trench coat gave him the air of a loping hound, harried, a little ungainly and ill at ease.

The boat that had brought him to the island turned round immediately to return to Manhattan, sketching a gentle ellipsis along the Hudson before it disappeared from view. It was the first time Logan had ever been to Ellis Island, although the sight of it in the bay was as familiar to him as it was to everyone. He bent over the body that the men had pulled from the water, which now lay on the pontoon deck. Routine. He said nothing, but after a brief examination he concluded that John Mitchell couldn't possibly have drowned. It was clear from the appearance of his face; and if there had been water in his lungs, his body would have blown up like a balloon. That was not what had happened. Casting a look at the tools lying on the ground, he guessed that the man had been electrocuted while repairing the light at the end of the dock. He surmised that the shock had made him lose his balance; his death likely resulted from the electrical surge and the subsequent fall into the icy water. Straightforward enough. He'd examine the body further tomorrow, in the quiet of the laboratory.

The men would have to come back over

the following days to remove the hundreds of crates of binders, the desks, tables, chairs, and beds that served no purpose here anymore. They'd have to do the inventory without the commissioner. And then they'd be back every day until the buildings were cleared. Right now, they were cold and hungry after a long morning, and not at all tickled by the presence of this stiff they were going to have to deliver that evening to the nearest morgue. And now this fella shows up, the coroner, peering into every corner without a word. All very peculiar.

Logan was making notes in a brown pad bound by an elastic band, with dog-eared pages and a leather loop to hold a pencil, underlining and circling various words, and drawing arrows between them.

A fine, icy rain began to fall. The Manhattan skyline disappeared into a halo of mist, making it seem as though the island was cut off from the rest of the world. Logan turned and entered the main building and, after wandering in various directions along the deserted corridors, headed for John Mitchell's office, where the light was still on. He closed the padded double door and glanced around the room. He could hear the men outside moving around, packing things up, hauling crates, shouting one another's names, getting aggravated when someone was clumsy or slack. The sound of their voices was muffled by the double doors. Logan walked towards the desk. It was warm in the office, it must have been the only room in the building that was properly heated. He took off his wet coat and set down his hat on the chair facing the desk. He noticed a pile of paper with a pen alongside it, bathed in the light of the brass desk lamp. He sighed, trying to chase away his fatigue, the weariness in his bones, and then sat down at Mitchell's desk on the high-backed wooden swivel chair, with the seat upholstered in cracked red leather.

The rest of the room was in perfect order. On a long table perpendicular to the desk was a row of dark-green binders fastened with fabric straps, their large white labels marked with black handwriting. Several keys, each with its own cardboard rectangle attached by a metal ring. Glass-fronted cabinets filled with binders and archive boxes, a label pinned to each piece of furniture. The mess in his own office flashed into Logan's mind, making him smile.

The pile of paper covered in handwriting sat in the middle of the table, as if its author had just left the room. Logan skimmed the last page, then turned the bundle over and started reading from the beginning. *Everything that follows took place at sea ...* The first page of each section of the diary, precisely dated, was neatly written, in careful, regular handwriting with well-spaced lines, but after two or three pages it changed. The rhythm of the writing became faster, too fast in places, the letters began to slope to the right, as if carried away by the weight of its writer's hand, the lines becoming cramped and the margins narrower, as if time or paper was about to run out. But each page was carefully numbered in the top right-hand corner with a figure inside a wobbly circle. Dates and times were noted with precision, as if this information served

as the ultimate marker, like bridges leading over a precipice. What surprised Logan
the most was that the whole thing was
written without any crossings out, as if its
author had known precisely what he was
going to say and had only to inscribe it on
the page.

Logan sighed. Damp permeated his
clothes. He lit a cigarette for warmth and
continued reading. Outside he could still
hear the thud of furniture being bumped
against the walls, the sound of boxes as
they slid across the wet tiles, shouts and
laughter from the men. The sounds faded
away. He sat and read the story of John
Mitchell, Liz, and Nella in the circle of light
thrown out by the lamp. He looked up and
noticed the pencil pot with the paper knife
sticking out, its blade pointing down. He
shifted the chair back and lit another cigarette. Beyond the halo of lamplight, there
was complete darkness. Suddenly he started.
Acqua e fuoco. Water and fire. He put down
the pages, stood up, and went to the window. Night, nothing but night. He began to
pace up and down the room, not knowing

where to look, trying to calm his heart that was beating too loud and too fast.

There was nothing more for him to do here. He sat down, then stood up again too quickly, and the chair rocked back with a crack of dry wood. He winced, then pulled on his trench, picked up the bundle of paper, and after a moment's hesitation, slipped it into the coat's inside pocket. He put on his hat and opened the door, beckoning to two of the men who were sitting on the stairs trying to shield themselves from the draft. *I'm done, you can empty this room and we can go.*

He needed something strong, something burning, to steady the feeling of disquiet that had taken hold of him. A face appeared to him in his exhaustion, in the muggy, oppressive, dusty gloom. Mary. Mary, who was waiting for him at home, Mary, who had taken to reproaching him, with increasing impatience, for always getting home from work so late; she was fed up and he knew it. He was so bad at talking. She smiled at him less and less when he arrived home, dog-tired, defeated;

she'd just look at him as he yanked off his tie, collapsed into an armchair, and downed a tumbler of whiskey. Mary, always so keen to talk, to tell him about her day, to listen to him talking about his, always waiting for an affectionate gesture, and he'd just sit there and close his eyes, wanting nothing more than to forget his day.

Sometimes in bed at night he'd reach for her, touch her stomach, feel the warmth of her body. More and more frequently now she would edge away or push his hand aside; gently, but all the same, and he didn't insist. Tonight he'd promised to be home early, but he hadn't been planning on a man being burned to a crisp while changing a bulb and ending up in the Hudson. Unlucky guy. Nor had he planned on finding these damn papers on the man's desk, containing a story that couldn't simply be sealed up in a box for posterity. There was too much love, too much pain on those pages. He told himself he'd make up for it at the weekend, he'd promise Mary a Sunday just the two of them, a movie, dinner in a restaurant, and, if it wasn't too cold, a walk in her beloved Central Park. He sighed and closed his eyes for a moment, picturing Mary's face in a frown, her forehead puckered; he didn't like the way it aged her. Sunday. I promise, Mary. Sunday. Promise.

It was late and he knew she'd be waiting for him. He had to get back to Manhattan, and then there was still the subway, a change of train, the exit. He'd buy her some roses if the guy at the flower stall on the corner outside the station was still there. Tired roses, tired like him, like Mary, like that guy whose life ended on the dock at the end of the island, two women lodged in his heart. He saw himself walking down the tree-lined side street and entering their apartment building. On the third floor, Mary would be waiting for him in her red dress, the one she looked so pretty in, her hair and face all dolled up, sitting despondently at the table laid for a meal long gone cold. He knew what he wanted to say to her. *Mary, don't be mad at me. A real strange thing happened today. Let me hold you.* He wanted to feel her skin, her hair, her arms, her back, her ass, squeeze her, crush her, try to pull her into him, completely inside him, to become one, because they were alive, yes, they were alive and that was the only thing that mattered.

Andrew Logan was the last to board the ferry. John Mitchell's body, covered with a gray blanket, had already been brought on. The engine was turning and there was a strong smell of diesel on the wind. The lights on Ellis Island had been switched off. He climbed aboard slowly, a slight swell making him steady himself, and the captain began to maneuver the boat clear of the dock. Direction Manhattan.

Logan went and stood at the back of the ferry, holding on to the rail and staring back at the island as it gradually faded from sight. He could still just about make out the four turrets and their onion domes and the white-painted facade, then the island seemed to dissolve in the darkness. He stared at the tip of his cigarette, the only thing still glowing in the dark, and the triangular wake fringed with white foam that trailed behind the ferry like a wire drawing him back to dry land. Behind him, the city stood tall in all its glory, with its neon signs and brightly lit windows. The febrile city in all its profusion, all that life, all that din, its sirens and klaxons. Logan felt the crumpled bundle of paper he had brought with him billowing under his trench coat. He tried one last time to make out the contours of the island. It had vanished, covered by night, as though a sheet had been laid over all the sorrows and regrets and memories of men, as if none of this had ever existed.

September 2012–January 2014

If there is one thing I learned from this strange adventure of writing, it is this, above all: the freedom of the author, as I have felt it, is not about inventing characters, situations, mysteries, but about listening to and welcoming the characters who came to meet me, each with his own individual story, enhanced by some of my own questions and obsessions.

A writer's freedom lies in the choice of whether or not to pursue these inexplicable encounters, and to give them life. So it was with *The Last Days of Ellis Island*.

In August 2012, I visited Ellis Island, now the Museum of Immigration, not far from the Statue of Liberty. It's hard to explain the overwhelming emotion I felt in this place, which today guards the memory of all those exiles. It's hard to explain the feeling of vertigo I experienced as I walked along the building's corridors and deserted staircases for hours on end, going from room to room, each one filled with objects, memories, and photographs.

Migrants, emigrants, immigrants. Transit. Words still charged with an acute resonance. A few weeks later, without having planned to or even wanting to write it, this story came into being.

All the characters in this novel are products of my imagination, apart from three. Nonetheless, I took liberties with their characters.

The first is Arne Peterssen, the Norwegian sailor, about whom only his name is known. He was the last immigrant to go through Ellis Island in November 1954, the day before the station closed. I allowed myself to invent his story.

Luigi Chianese, the Italian interpreter, did not exist, but I took some details of his career (though neither characteristics or actions, all of which are entirely fictitious) from that of Fiorello La Guardia (1882–1947), who worked as an interpreter at Ellis, before becoming a lawyer and then mayor of New York (1934–1945). One of the city's airports is named after him.

August Sherman (1865–1925) was indeed

employed at Ellis Island. He held the position of Chief Registry Clerk, and between 1905 and 1925 he took some two hundred and fifty photographs of newly arrived immigrants, many of which can be seen at the museum. Little is known about him and the details of his character and activities are my own invention.

They reflect my shock as I stood in front of all these faces, captured at a moment that must have been for each one of them as much an ordeal as a new beginning. I stood and imagined the stories of all these people whose fates had been reduced to mere anthropological documents. The portraits were indeed published in journals for anti-immigration racial propaganda purposes, though the precise role played by Sherman in this process is unknown.

Since then, the human and historical dimension of these portraits has been restored, rendering these women and men their dignity at last. It is the least that they are owed.

NATASHA LEHRER is a writer and literary translator based in France. She writes features and book reviews for a variety of newspapers including *The Guardian*, *The Times*, and *The Observer*. Some of her recent translations are *A Call for Revolution* by the Dalai Lama, *Chinese Spies* by Roger Faligot, Victor Segalen's *Journey to the Land of the Real*, and *Memories of Low Tide* by Chantal Thomas. Lehrer won a Rockower Award for Journalism in 2016, and in 2017 was awarded the Scott Moncrieff Translation Prize for her co-translation of *Suite for Barbara Loden* by Nathalie Léger.

On the Design

As book design is an integral part of the reading experience, we would like to acknowledge the work of those who shaped the form in which the story is housed.

Tessa van der Waals (Netherlands) is responsible for the cover design, cover typography, and art direction of all World Editions books. She works in the internationally renowned tradition of Dutch Design. Her bright and powerful visual aesthetic maintains a harmony between image and typography and captures the unique atmosphere of each book. She works closely with internationally celebrated photographers, artists, and letter designers. Her work has frequently been awarded prizes for Best Dutch Book Design.

The cover photograph was taken in 1905 by the pioneering social photographer Lewis W. Hine (1874–1940), who was drawn to Ellis Island and the "new immigration," a term used to describe the waves of newcomers from Southern and Eastern Europe. Hine photographed at the immigration station between 1904 and 1909. The woman in the photograph was an immigrant from Italy. The black-and-white original has been colored in for use on this cover.